Haunts and Howls Collections

Haunts and Howls and Guardian Spells
Haunts and Howls Where Demons Dwell
Haunts and Howls and Jesters Bells

HAUNTS AND HOWLS AND JESTERS BELLS

A CONTEMPORARY FANTASY COLLECTION

KAT SIMONS

HAUNTS AND HOWLS AND JESTERS BELLS
Copyright © 2023 by Katrina Tipton
All rights reserved.

Published 2023 by T&D Publishing
Cover design: © 2023 T&D Publishing
Cover art: © Piolka | Dreamstime.com
Interior book design © 2023 T&D Publishing
ISBN-13: 978-1-944600-74-7 (Trade Paperback Edition)
ISBN-13: 978-1-944600-75-4 (Large Print Edition)

This book is licensed for your personal enjoyment only. All rights reserved. No part of this book may be reproduced, scanned, or distributed in any print or electronic form without written permission from the author, excepting brief quotes used in the context of a review.

This is a work of fiction. All of the characters, places, organizations, and events portrayed are either products of the author's imagination or are used fictitiously. Any resemblance to actual persons, living or dead, business establishments, events, or locales is entirely coincidental.

First printing T&D Publishing edition: October 2023
For information, contact T&D Publishing:
https://www.tanddpublishing.com

HAUNTS AND HOWLS AND JESTERS BELLS

CONTENTS

Introduction	xi
THREE BELLS RINGING	1
I JUST ATE A BUG	43
BORED QUESTLESS	53
TING LING	81
SOPHIE SAVES THE WORLD	105
HOURGLASS THROUGH THE CATS EYES	147
Thank You	207
THE TROUBLE WITH BLACK CATS AND DEMONS Excerpt	209
Books By Kat Simons	223
More Books By Kat Simons	227
About the Author	229

*For my mom. Who shares my sense of humor.
And to my family, for keeping me laughing.*

INTRODUCTION

The Haunts and Howls collections are my ode to spooky season every year. October, Halloween, all of it is just a lot of fun for me. But as well as all things spooky, I also like a good light, humorous story. And the theme for this year fits that combination perfectly.

Jesters are, traditionally, supposed to be about humor and entertainment. Whether eliciting big laughs or quiet chuckles or exchanging bawdy banter, jesters were there to make their audiences laugh. That's where the humor of this year's theme comes in. The funny aspect of the jester character.

But then we get to the fact that jesters are, in essence, clowns. And clowns are terrifying. No, really. They are terrifying.

To be honest, I didn't get the "clowns are terrifying" thing completely until college. My grandmother hated them, and I didn't understand why. I wasn't crazy about them, but scary? Na, no, not really.

Well! I was wrong.

First, Stephen King and his infamous Pennywise from IT set me on the path to seeing the creepiness in clowns. I was primed by that novel, open to the idea that clowns could be really scary. Then I get to college. I'm living on a tall hill that's extremely steep, and my only mode of transportation is a small moped that couldn't go over twenty-nine miles an hour. The road straight up this hill was impossible for my moped, so I had to take the switchback road that wound more slowly up to the top where our house was (I was living with a bunch of other college students; the house wasn't fancy).

One day, on my way up this slow, winding hill, I pass the direct road going down and there, in a small car filled to bursting with balloons, was the most angry-looking clown I had ever seen. Scowling, snarling, in full makeup and costume. Just really angry looking. And the makeup was reminiscent of Pennywise. He was driving down the hill, looking like he wanted to murder someone. I continued up the hill, freaked out, but figuring he was a birthday clown and he'd had a bad day.

But then! As I'm coming around the corner, higher on the hill, who do I see again? That's it. The clown. *Still driving down the hill*! I hadn't seen him pass me to go back uphill to reach this spot, though. He was just suddenly there at a spot higher on the hill, still driving down the steep road.

And this time, he doesn't ignore me. This time, I get the full impact of his glare as I toddle past on my little pink moped. He *glared* at me like something was very much my fault.

I have never looked at a clown the same way again.

Now, I know, reasonably, there were plenty of logical explanations for that encounter. Simple ones, like he was trying to find a house and couldn't. That I'd missed him driving up the steep hill as I came around one of the switchbacks. I know there was a logical explanation. Didn't make that clown any less creepy.

INTRODUCTION

Thus, my "clowns are terrifying" opinion.

And what's better than scary creepy clowns in a Haunts and Howls collection, right?

To be honest, I didn't go with full-on clowns in any of these stories. I didn't want to be that on the nose. The closest I got was the very first story. Mostly, I just added creepy and/or funny elements to these stories to fit the theme.

To start, though, I do want to admit right up front that because humor is really subjective, what I find laugh-out-loud funny might fall flat for someone else. And to make things worse, I have a slightly weird sense of humor, which I share with my mother, so I come by it honestly. So you're forewarned, the humor here will either hit your funny bone, or it won't. For a reference point on this, while I would never compare my skills to the late, great Sir Terry Pratchett who is my absolute icon for humorous fantasy, my attempts at humor do fall into that sort of dry, absurdist sort of vein. Hopefully, even if we do not share a sense of humor, these stories will entertain either way.

With all that said, I start the collection with a super creepy story without any humor at all (back to that "clowns are terrifying" point).

If you've read HAUNTS AND HOWLS WHERE DEMONS DWELL, you might remember a story called *Friday's Curious Shop*, my homage to an 1980s horror TV series I used to love as a teenager. Since writing that first story, I knew I wanted to write more set at Friday's Curious (not curios—curious) Shop, and this theme felt perfect for one of those stories. *Three Bells Ringing* is probably the creepiest story in the entire collection, so we're starting right off with the haunts and the howls.

The second story in the collection is one that I find amusing (so does my mother, so now you know what we think is funny). The title comes from a line in one of my favorite movies from back in the day. *Overboard*, the original staring Goldie Hawn and Kurt Russell. There's a scene where Goldie Hawn, as a snooty rich woman who's lost her memory, is riding in the back of the hero's truck, and she says, sort of choking on the words, "I just…ate a bug." To this day, this line makes my mom and me (and my sister for that matter) giggle. It's all in the delivery. Goldie's comedic chops cannot be denied.

Anyway, thirty years later, I'm mulling over something completely different, and that line pops into my head. And with it, an entire story. I was supposed to be writing something else that day. Instead, I wrote *I Just Ate a Bug*.

Which is a story that's hard to follow. So I followed it with another one that I find funny. This one more in the high fantasy humor vein. Still on the silly side, and I hope entertaining. The original version of *Bored Questless* was written years ago. Probably twenty-five years ago at this stage. It has been completely rewritten for this collection. But anyone who's heard of or read anything by my alter ego, Isabo Kelly, might remember the first version of this story, which I had up at her website many moons ago.

And, you might ask, did my mother also find *this* story funny? In its original form, she loved it so much, she drew fan art for it.

Next up, we move to something…a little harder to explain without giving any of it away. *Ting Ling* can fall into the creepy end of the spectrum pretty easily, but maybe a little humor there, too? I'll leave it to the reader to judge. And I won't say any more about it for fear of spoiling the story.

Sophie Saves the World also started its original journey years ago. Like almost everything I write that I find funny, this one started with a sudden idea, a spark of something truly absurd occurring to me, and a story spun out from there. In this case, it was the idea of being in the bathroom, stuck on the toilet, when something very extraordinary happens that had nothing to do with bathroom activities. You'll know what I mean within the first paragraph.

You might also notice a similar theme in *Sophie Saves the World* and *Bored Questless*, but with a different take. I was going to say more here but that might give the ending of Sophie's story away, so this hint is the most I'll admit.

And finally, I finish the collection with another sequel to a previous Haunts and Howls story. The first Destiny Cats novella appeared in the collection, HAUNTS AND HOWLS AND GUARDIAN SPELLS. *Destiny Through the Cats Eyes* introduced a set of characters I knew had a lot more stories in them. And now, the Destiny Cats are back! This time on a new adventure in *Hourglass Through the Cats Eyes*. While this novella falls more along the scary adventure end of the spectrum for this book, if you know cats, you'll probably also find parts of this one funny.

Spanning the spectrum from creepy to funny to scary fun… I hope readers will enjoy this newest collection in the Haunts and Howls series. And if we do end up sharing a sense of humor, please feel free to let me know! It's nice to know it's not just me and my mom.

Kat Simons
October 2023

THREE BELLS RINGING

A FRIDAY'S CURIOUS SHOP STORY

CHAPTER ONE

Working in Friday's Curious Shop had introduced Riley Anderson to a lot of unusual people and a lot of unusual things. She hadn't even been working in this secondhand store for very long. A few months, according to the regular pay deposited into her bank account every two weeks.

When she bothered to stop and think about it, Riley didn't really remember applying for the job here at Friday's, or getting it. She had some vague memories of being unemployed and worried about meeting rent. Worried the three people she shared the small two-bedroom apartment she called home would kick her out if she couldn't get work. She'd thought she might end up homeless, at least, she thought that had been a worry. Riley didn't have any backups, any family to help when things got tough. So being out of a job really would have been bad.

But all that seemed like distant memories now. She was aware of having only worked in Friday's for a limited period of time because she felt like there was still a lot she was learning. At the same time, it felt like she'd been here for years.

And yet, there was always something new, something interesting to uncover. A quiet retail job that involved a lot of dusting probably should have been boring. It wasn't. Riley *liked* being here. Her bosses, the brother and sister owners of the store, Doreen and Ian Sinclair, were good bosses. They gave her responsibilities and were nice. Easy to talk to when they were around. Well, Doreen could be a little reticent. She never talked about things outside of the store. But Ian was chatty and liked to discuss the things he picked up at auctions and estate sales for the store.

Friday's was full of things that, on a good day, might have been considered antiques, but mostly just a load of stuff that other people didn't want anymore. A treasure trove if you were willing to navigate the piled high tables, stacks of crates, awkwardly placed shelves, and never-ending dust to dig up those treasures.

One of the most important things she'd learned since starting here was that one person's treasure was another person's junk. The other most important thing was not to go into the back storage room without Doreen or Ian escorting her.

Even a few months of working at Friday's had been enough time to meet some of the more interesting residents of New York City. Though how they found this place off a small side street in a section of Queens not known for its foot traffic, Riley was never sure. People just wandered in, like the store was located in the middle of a shopping district instead of tucked away near the elevated subway tracks, surrounded by storage facilities and truck rental places. The building itself didn't look like much from the outside. More like a warehouse than a retail space. Though it did have large windows with stuff piled up against them. And the charming wooden sign over the door announced it as a retail store.

Friday's Curious—not curios, curious—Shop was what some might consider a hidden gem. On good days, when it was sunny out and Ian brought them sandwiches from the good sandwich place a few blocks away, she considered the store a hidden gem, too.

But occasionally, the strange and interesting people who managed to find Friday's were…not the kind of people Riley would voluntarily talk to if she hadn't been working here. Sometimes, she wasn't even sure why she found someone strange. An instinct maybe. Just that sometimes, someone came into the shop and they gave her the creeps.

This particular customer was one of those people.

"Can I help you?" Riley asked in her best customer service voice.

The man had walked into the store about ten minutes earlier, ringing the little bell over the glass front door. Doreen had told Riley during her first week at work that it was best to let people wander around a bit before offering help. This was the kind of place people liked to dig through, and they didn't always like dealing with staff. So Riley always gave people a few minutes to wander. And if they looked like they were searching for something specific, she'd offer to help.

This customer seemed to be hunting for something in particular, not just wandering around looking at all the potential treasures amid the piles of used toys in the wooden and plastic crates and inside the display case where he'd spent most of his time so far.

When he turned to face her, his smile instantly gave her the creeps. She tried not to judge people by their appearance because she'd seen how that could backfire. One of her roommates had dated the most gorgeous man, only to have him turn out to be a jerk. Another had dated an equally gorgeous man who turned out to be lovely and weirdly humble. And Lauren was dating two people who were pretty ordinary looking and each of them were pleasant, with a sexiness that grew on you.

Looks didn't mean much in Riley's experience. But this guy…

That smile made her gut tighten and she took an involuntary step backward before she could stop herself. There were a lot of teeth in that smile. White teeth that gleamed in the overhead florescent lights.

She forced her own smile to cover her reaction, but she didn't move closer to the man. She wasn't alone in the shop. She was never alone in the shop. At the moment, Ian was in the back storage room and Doreen was in the cramped little office behind the cash register desk. So there were people within shouting distance if she needed them.

The fact that she was worried she might have to shout for help wasn't lost on her.

"Looking for anything in particular," she said, forcing a professionalism she wasn't feeling. Her gut was so tight she was feeling that breakfast wrap Ian had treated her to. And her pulse pounded hard enough she was afraid it was visible in her neck. The rapid thump of her heartbeat made her want to put a hand to her chest to slow it down. Sweat broke out along her spine.

Riley was aware this was all a very over-the-top reaction to a smile. But she had no control over it. Her logical mind had nothing to do with this. This was all lizard brain fear.

"I'm looking for a hat," the man said.

His voice was surprisingly pleasant after the fear invoked by his smile. Mild and with a nice clip to the end of his words, like he'd had vocal training. One of Lauren's current romantic partners was an actor and this customer had that same kind of cadence.

Hearing him speak broke some of the shock his smile had caused and she was able to take in the rest of him finally. Not particularly old, though not young. Maybe mid-forties but a well-preserved mid-forties, with very few lines in his artificially tanned skin. His blond hair was thinning but he hid it well with a good cut. He had a long, pointed chin and high cheekbones, and brown eyes that were a little too close together over a short, wide nose. None of his features went together very well, but not in an obvious way.

He was dressed for the warmer spring weather, in short-sleeved, white, button-down shirt, and slacks in a bright red color that Ian would have admired. He wasn't carrying any bags or backpacks, so his hands were free. No glasses, no jewelry except for a single ring on his left pinky finger. The ring was a thick silver with a pattern on it she couldn't see, but the metal caught the overhead light the same way as the man's teeth had and that made her quickly look away from the ring.

"A winter hat? Summer hat? Baseball cap? Children's hat?" She forced another smile. "We have a wide variety."

"I've noticed," the man said. "I'm looking for something very specific, though. A jester's hat."

"A jester's hat?"

"Crushed velvet, green and white, split into three points. Bells on the ends of each point."

Riley nodded, but didn't immediately comment. Jesters weren't her favorite things. They were related to clowns. And clowns weren't her favorite thing either. She wasn't as terrified of them as her grandmother. But she didn't like them. They were creepy more often than they were funny in her opinion.

But the hat the man was looking for didn't sound like something they had. "I'm not sure I've seen anything like that here, I'm afraid."

"Maybe in the back?" He folded his hands in front of him and his mouth stretched in what was probably supposed to be a smile, but the expression just made Riley's insides tight and uncomfortable.

"How about I ask one of my bosses," she said by way of an excuse to get away from that smile. "I'll be right back."

"The Sinclairs are here?" he asked.

And for some reason, the fact that he knew the who Ian and Doreen were made Riley antsy. It shouldn't have been. If he knew her bosses, it meant he came in her regularly, was a regular customer. She was sure this place had those, even though she hadn't met any since starting. That she knew of. But a store like this, not located on a regular foot traffic route, had to have regulars to even stay in business, right?

So this man, whoever he was, was probably one of those regulars. And as such, she needed to be courteous. But also, she really didn't want to be around him anymore.

"They are," she said. "I'll just check. Maybe they've seen something like what you're looking for."

"Thank you," the man said. Then he turned to the toys he'd been looking at.

For reasons that she would have had a hard time explaining, Riley backed away from the man, not wanting to turn her back on him until she absolutely had to. She was well behind the cover of a taller glass cabinet filled with music boxes when she finally turned around and hurried toward the office to talk to Doreen.

She couldn't go into the storage room looking for Ian, which was unfortunate because having the large man here would be reassuring. Maybe Doreen could call him to the front of the store. Riley felt a little silly for her reaction. The man looking for the jester's hat hadn't been threatening, even a little bit. He hadn't crowded her or made any aggressive moves. He'd smiled and been polite. These were not the acts of a man she needed to worry about.

Except she was worried about him. And even if that didn't make a lot of sense in the circumstances, she decided to err on the side of cautions. Erring on the side of caution had saved her butt on a few occasions.

She ducked around the tall wooden desk that served as the checkout counter, and contemplated the storage room door directly behind it. A curl of some urge, a push to go back there coiled around her chest. She flexed her hands into fists, relaxed them. Then went to the office door off to the left to get Doreen.

She hadn't been in the storage room very much since starting work here. She'd learned her lesson on the first day that it wasn't a place she wanted to hazard without an escort. It didn't seem like it should be as large, or as confusing as it was. There didn't seem, from the outside, to be enough building for the sheer length and breadth of space occupied by the storage room. And while the standing shelves seemed to be arranged in neat, orderly rows, it was really easy to get mixed up between rows. Getting lost among the stacks was all too possible. And the last thing she needed to do was get fired because she'd gotten lost in the backroom and left a customer unattended in the front of the store.

Especially one that gave her the creeps for reasons surpassing logic.

She knocked on the closed office door and waited for Doreen to say, "Enter!" before she pushed it open.

Like the rest of the store, the office was an odd arrangement of clutter and organization. There were sturdy wooden shelves with various items from the store that needed repairs placed seemingly at random against one wall. There was an orderly row of tall, gray metal filing cabinets against another wall, their drawers neatly labeled with letters. Until the last filing cabinet which was labeled with numbers. Numbers that didn't appear to have any obvious order to them, though, like the lettered drawers that went in alphabetical order.

Unlike the rest of the store, there wasn't the combination of dust and cleaning polish smell back here. Despite how often Riley dusted and rearranged things in the front, the sheer quantity of stuff meant there was always the smell of old things and dust. She didn't mind. She liked the smell of old things. And thanks to her new bottle of allergy medicine, she could even tolerate the dust without sneezing constantly.

But that smell didn't extend into the office. Back here, the scent of Doreen's favorite tea—Earl Gray from a place in Manhattan—and Ian's favorite coffee—Chocolate Macadamia Nut he had specially delivered from Hawaii— dominated. The two flavors of drinks conflicted a little, so the room didn't necessarily smell great. But it was an ordinary, office smell that overrode any dust buildup.

There was a small wooden desk with an old-fashioned roll top against the back wall of the office, with a lot of little cubby holes inside the roll top, with three larger drawers on either side of the base of the desk. A modern, comfortably soft, black microfiber chair sat before the desk. And a small three-legged, tall wooden stool to one side. The stool reminded Riley of some of the more rickety stools from the bar right around the corner from her apartment where she'd gone for drinks with her roommates right after moving in. The only time they'd ever been social together.

Doreen sat in the comfortable chair, but had swiveled

around to face the door, which was at her back when sitting at the desk. For some reason, Riley found that arrangement uncomfortable. She wasn't sure she'd be able to work in here with her back to the door, but she wasn't entirely sure why that idea bothered her.

Doreen Sinclair was a pretty woman of indeterminant age, with good skin, pale and freckled. She had a riot of curly red hair that she kept pulled off her face with hairbands that broke frequently in their quests to contain the heavy mass. Her thick glasses, with a solid brown plastic frame, gave her brown eyes a distinctive look that Riley had always liked. Unlike her brother's more flamboyant fashion sense, Doreen was dressed in one of her usual long, plain skirts, this one a simple brown corduroy material, with a long-sleeved, button-up cotton shirt that was the closest she seemed to come to accommodating the warmer weather as they moved through spring.

There was an air-conditioner running in the office that made goosebumps rise on Riley's bare arms. She figured that's why Doreen insisted on long sleeves.

Riley cleared her throat and rubbed at the goosebumps to warm her skin. "We have a customer looking for a specific hat, and I told him I'd ask you about it. It isn't something I've seen in here before, but he wanted me to check."

"What kind of hat?" Doreen pushed her thick-lensed glasses up her nose.

"A jester's hat."

Doreen sat up straighter, leaning forward slightly. "Did he describe something specific, or just a general jester's hat?"

"He was very specific." Riley described the hat the man had asked for.

"With bells. He was specific about it having bells?"

Riley nodded. Didn't most of those kinds of weird jester

hats have bells on the ends? She was no expert, though. Maybe there was something important about the bells?

"He also seems to know you and Ian. He asked if 'the Sinclairs' were here. Or, well, when I said I was going to ask my bosses about the hat, he confirmed you were here."

Doreen nodded, but her gaze was turned inward. "Is he still out there?"

"He looked like he intended to wait when I came back."

"I'll get Ian. Go keep the man occupied until we get there." Doreen stood abruptly and hurried past Riley without any further explanation.

Which wasn't entirely unusual but was strange enough to make Riley nervous. She really didn't want to spend any more time with that man on her own.

All this over a jester's hat. And Doreen hadn't even said if they had the hat or not.

Damn. Now what was Riley going to say to the customer?

CHAPTER TWO

*R*iley found him still hovering in the children's toy section. Well, loosely the children's toy section. The place wasn't that well organized. But they'd tried to put similar things in the same general area as often as possible.

As she rounded a rack of old dress shirts, Riley spotted the man studying the music boxes inside the free-standing glass cabinet. He smiled at her when she approached. This time, the smile looked more ordinary. Not the stretching of lips that had so creeped her out earlier.

"You have a nice collection here. This pink inlaid one is particularly lovely."

Riley glanced at the case. The pink one in question had a pretty gloss painted over the wooden side panels, was decorated with silver filagree, and the open lid revealed a dark red, crushed velvet interior with a ballerina in a white tutu, her hands raised to her sides. Riley couldn't remember if the music in that one still worked. But it was a pretty box.

"Are you interested in getting a closer look?" she asked, forcing the professional tone and trying not to make it obvious she didn't want to get too close to the man. Even with the more ordinary smile, she wasn't eager to stand right next to him.

"No, thank you. Maybe later. Did the Sinclairs say if they had the hat or not?"

"Doreen is getting Ian now. They're checking in the back."

The man's dark eyes widened slightly and something like a flare of light brightened in the depths. A kind of bluish green color that Riley assumed was a trick of the overhead lighting.

Because standing around awkwardly didn't feel very professional and she felt like she was out here to keep an eye on the man and not let him wander around long unattended, she started down the path of small talk. Which wasn't her forte, but a few months of working retail had helped a little.

"So a jester's hat is an unusual collector's item? Are you a collector?"

"You could say that." The smile was bland. His gaze moved between her and some toy boxes he made a show of examining.

"Just jester hats? Or anything to do with jesters and clowns?" She really wasn't crazy about clowns. She'd have preferred another topic of conversation. Good thing her gran wasn't here.

"I'm looking for this particular hat. Specifically."

"For a…costume? Or is it a special hat worn by someone famous?"

She was reaching here. Really, she'd be surprised if something in here was really valuable, but that was the thing about secondhand items. Sometimes the most ordinary looking things turned out to be worth a small fortune to the right person, with the right interest, and the right expertise. And she wasn't an expert in most of this stuff. Her experience with secondhand stores before this was as a customer interesting in bargains and old things that she could afford.

"Actually," the man said, turning to face her fully, his expression thoughtful, "the hat did once belong to someone. A great magician."

"Like, he had a show in Vegas or…?"

The corner of the man's mouth ticked, but Riley couldn't tell if it was a smile or not. "He…didn't make Vegas. But he was an impressive magician. Rumor has it, he stored some of his power in the hat."

"Power?" Riley shifted from one foot to the other. Where were Doreen and Ian?

"Magic. Quite impressive magic. So the story goes. Apparently, he made some sort of deal, with dark gods, and they gave him the magic in exchange for his soul."

"Sounds like a bad deal," she said, unable to look away from the man. That weird green-blue light flared in his eyes again. She'd never seen the overhead lighting do that to anyone's eyes before.

"Depends on your perspective," the man said. "Sometimes the cost of the soul is worth the prize."

"What prize? Just some magic for tricks and things?"

"Power is power. Many people crave it."

"Weird."

His mouth ticked again, and this time the smile formed. Not the creepy smile, though. Not even his neutrally polite one. This one was amused. "It's just a story, of course. Take of it what you will."

"What kind of power? In a jester's hat?"

The man shrugged and turned away from her. Riley blinked hard a few times as a wave of dizziness washed through her. She pressed her hand to a nearby table until the wave passed.

"Who knows," the man said, his attention on an old-fashioned wooden gameboard with holes in it filled with little colorful wooden balls. "The stories are varied. Some say the power was to control other people. Some say the hat made the wearer a king. Some say the magic made people laugh until they died."

"Sounds like a weird way to die," she said as her head stopped swimming and she got her balance back. Because looking at the man left her uncomfortable, she turned to a nearby table covered in baby clothes and started folding and rearranging. Anything to keep her hands busy and her attention on something other than the customer.

"I imagine it would be," the man said. "There's another story that claims the hat is cursed. That the original owner, when he sacrificed his soul to the dark gods, was cursed to… occupy the hat after he was killed."

"Killed? Not just died of old age, huh? Suppose that happens a lot when you make deals with dark gods, huh?"

"Absolutely."

From the corner of her eye, Riley saw the man's amused smile again.

"The story goes, once he was killed, his essence became a part of the hat, and anyone willing to wear the hat will be cursed, too."

"What kind of curse? Just…soaked into the hat after they die?"

"Not quite."

Noise from the back of the store brought the strange conversation to an end. Both Riley and the man turned to face the noise. Riley found her heartbeat thumping hard and she wasn't even sure why.

But the entire episode had her weirded out, and Riley really needed other people here now.

CHAPTER THREE

Doreen was the first to come into view, navigating around the various tables and standing shelves toward them. She wasn't carrying anything obvious. Certainly not a jester's hat.

The man stepped forward at Doreen's approach, but Riley saw his shoulders slump when it was clear she wasn't carrying the hat.

"Good afternoon," Doreen greeted the man. "Welcome to Friday's. You're looking for a jester hat? A specific one, or will any one do?"

"A specific one," the man said, his gaze narrowing.

Riley had sort of assumed Doreen would know the man, since he seemed to know who the Sinclair siblings were. But neither showed any hint that they recognized each other.

"My brother is going through our inventory. But maybe you can describe what you're looking for to me. In case I missed anything in translation."

Riley raised a brow at Doreen, who ignored the look, her full attention on the customer.

The man went on to describe the same jester's hat he had

for Riley. In fact, he described it in exactly the same wording. Exactly. Like he'd memorized the words and was repeating them verbatim.

"Crushed velvet, green and white, split into three points. Bells on the ends of each point."

"Silver or gold bells?" Doreen asked.

The man blinked. Like he hadn't expected that question. "Silver."

"You're sure?"

"Yes."

Doreen narrowed her eyes and clucked her tongue against her teeth. "I do think I've seen something like that in the back. Hopefully, my brother will locate it. Is there any other similar item that might suit as a substitute? I know we have a hat with four points in yellow, blue and green. It's not exactly what you're looking for but close."

"No. It has to be this specific hat." At Doreen's raised brows, the man straightened and deployed the friendly, not creepy smile. "It's for a collector. He has a lot of jester's hats and is specific about this one for his collection. I check at any of the secondhand stores I come across."

"I see."

But Riley didn't. She frowned at the man. He made it sound like he'd just wandered in here off the street and was just checking. But he'd known who the Sinclairs were. Earlier, he'd given the impression he knew exactly what specific store he was in.

While she wasn't keen on seeing his creepy smile again, Riley sort of hoped he flashed it at Doreen, so Riley would know she wasn't going crazy. Doreen was hard to freak out. She had a high tolerance for weird and strange. And...well, really strange.

Riley had vague memories of the day she came in to

apply for this job and something strange happening with a customer but most of what had happened had faded away so all she really remembered now was a dust up that resulted in having to put the store back together over some item a customer had wanted but the Sinclairs weren't prepared to sell to him.

At the time, though, Riley *did* remember thinking it was all pretty scary. Since then, she was convinced both the siblings were good at handling weird stuff, so she hadn't thought much more about that first incident.

This particular customer fit into the weird category for Riley. She just couldn't put her finger on why. If Doreen got the same vibe from him, at least Riley would know she wasn't imagining things.

Except...

Maybe she was. Maybe that initial reaction to the man was pure imagination. A trick of light and shadow. Maybe it was being in the old toys section of the store. Maybe she'd imagined the man's disturbing smile and the flash of light in his eyes.

"I'm sorry," Doreen said suddenly with a bright smile of her own. "I didn't get your name."

"Thaddeus. Thaddeus Eckland."

"Mr. Eckland." Doreen gave a little head bob of acknowledgement. "And your friend's name? If you don't mind sharing."

Eckland answered after a beat that was almost too short a pause for Riley to notice. "Jefferson. James Jefferson."

"Excellent alliteration."

"His father thought so."

"Has he collected a lot of jester's hats." Doreen moved into the sort of stalling small talk that kept customers occupied during a wait.

Riley stood to one side, awkwardly wondering if she should leave or stay. She honestly didn't want to leave Doreen alone with the man. Any more than she'd wanted to be alone with him herself. But there was really no reason for the both of them to hover around Mr. Eckland while they waited on Ian.

If there'd been other customers, Riley would have left to help someone else. As it was, Mr. Thaddeus Eckland was the only person in the store. So that was Riley's excuse to stay. She did move a little away from the two and started rearranging a shelf with board games on it. The table where the games were stacked gave her a good view toward the back of the store, the direction Ian would be coming from.

She kept waiting for Eckland to tell Doreen about the hat's supposed curse, or any of the stories he'd regaled Riley with. But he didn't mention any of the magic and curse stuff. He talked about his friend having about a dozen of the jester's hats in various sizes and shapes, and being very interested in this specific one for his collection.

"Not sure I've heard of this one before," Doreen said. "Which is surprising. I would have thought, if it was special, it would have been something we'd heard of."

Everything she'd just said sounded like a lie to Riley. Did it to the man?

Riley glanced at him closer. His eyes were a little narrowed, but not obviously. His gaze was intent on Doreen. But his expression didn't otherwise give anything away.

"Perhaps you have to be very into jesters," Eckland said with a shrug.

"Probably," Doreen said. She pushed her glasses up as she held Eckland's gaze. "I have heard of some very interesting marotte, thought to be lucky and/or owned by some of the more famous medieval court jesters."

"Sounds interesting. I'm not the collector, though. My friend is. But I'll ask him if he has any good stories."

"Marotte?" Riley asked. Then sort of wished she hadn't when both Doreen and Eckland swung their attention to her. She could have just waited and Googled it.

"The staff or stick that a jester carries as part of the costume," Doreen said. "A prop."

"It's a comedic representation of a royal scepter," Eckland added. "Often with a carved face or head at the top."

"Sounds a little creepy."

Eckland smiled faintly. "They can be." He turned back to Doreen. "Do you have any interesting marotte on hand?"

"Nothing currently for sale," Doreen said.

Very precisely said. Not that they didn't have any. But that they weren't selling any they might have. Interesting enough to peak Riley's curiosity. Not interesting enough for her to ask the question in front of Mr. Eckland again.

"Shame." Eckland spread his hands in a slight shrug. "But it's really the hats that my friend collects. And he's been looking for this particular hat for a long time."

"And how did you get our names?"

Ah! Doreen finally asked one of the questions nagging at Riley.

Eckland raised his eyebrows and Doreen said, "We aren't exactly Christy's here and not known dealing for jester paraphernalia. I was just wondering how you happened on our place." She smiled. "Helps with our advertising efforts to know what's working."

Advertising? Did they do advertising for this place? Riley hadn't thought so. If they did, it seemed like it might be a waste of money since there were never that many customers in the place.

"Work acquaintance who's local," Eckland said. "I'm just in town for a conference. He recommended your store."

"How very kind of him. Does he have a name? I'd like to thank him the next time he comes in. Word of mouth keeps small businesses like ours running."

Eckland's shoulders seemed to tighten, and two deep lines formed around his mouth as his lips compressed. "I only know him by a ridiculous nickname. Nothing you'd recognize." Another shrug but this one all shoulders and jerky muscle movement.

"Fair enough."

Doreen seemed like she might ask another question when sound from the direction of the checkout desk made her pause. She glanced over her shoulder. "That sounds like Ian. I wonder if he found anything."

So did Riley.

She hoped the store made a sale even if she did find this customer creepy. Every sale was good and helped. At least, she thought they did. So few customers had to mean not a lot of money coming in. But the Sinclairs never seemed worried about money, or about the business making a profit. And Riley's pay was always deposited on time.

Huh. She'd never really thought about that before. How the hell did the Sinclairs make enough money to stay in business?

She was disrupted from her musings by the second Sinclair sibling walking around the music box display case.

Carrying a green and white, crushed velvet jester's hat.

CHAPTER FOUR

Ian Sinclair was a huge man. Not overweight. Just tall and broad shouldered. When Riley had first seen him, her initial impression had been of a bear moving through the shop. He was remarkably graceful for a man that size, and somehow managed to move around all the stacks of stuff and piled-high tables without knocking anything off. Riley, at three-quarters his size, never managed that with such ease.

He also dressed more elaborately than his sister. Today, his red checked trousers were polyester instead of tweed, in deference to the warmer temperatures, and his button-down shirt was a grayish color that picked up one of the details in the trousers. He wore an embroidered vest with a red and blue tartan pattern on it, which Riley thought looked too warm for the day, but Ian loved his vests. She wasn't sure she'd ever seen him without one.

The outfit probably shouldn't have worked. Especially on a large man with thick red hair and a full beard and mustache. Riley was no expert, but she'd read somewhere that most redheads couldn't wear red clothing well. Somehow, Ian made everything work, though, and whoever his vest tailor was, they were a genius, because Ian's vests always fit his large frame immaculately.

Riley highly doubted Thaddeus Eckland noticed Ian's fashion sense, though. The man's dark eyes had widened the minute Ian appeared carrying the jester's hat. And a little drip of sweat tracked down his cheek. Doreen had moved to one side of the music box cabinet, giving her brother room amidst the crowded tables and stacks of old toys. Riley also found herself shifting positions, moving just a little bit farther back and to one side so she was standing more behind Eckland than next to him.

Several seconds ticked by before she realized she'd moved in a way to block Eckland from the front door. Why had she done that? Did she think he'd grab the hat and bolt? And what if he did? Was the hat worth a lot of money? Maybe it was, since it had been in the back.

Still, the instinct to keep Eckland from "escaping" seemed weird in the circumstance. Strange enough, she almost returned to where she'd been. Then Eckland started talking and she just…stayed in place. Moving might mean drawing attention and she did not want to draw his attention in that moment.

Something in his voice sounded weirdly strained and harsh.

"That's it," Eckland said. "That's the hat. How long have you had it?"

"Don't know," Ian said. "Things build up here over time. Hard to say when anything arrives."

Riley frowned. While the main floor of the store seemed like chaos incarnate and that there was no way anyone would know everything here, she knew for a fact that everything in the back was kept in very precise inventories files. Including dates when things came into the store. She'd never asked why they kept such detailed inventory for the storage room stuff and were less specific about most of the front room stuff. It had never even occurred to her to ask.

But maybe Ian wanted to barter and drive the price of the hat up, create some mystery around it. Honestly, she wasn't sure what was happening here. She just got the impression that what was being said aloud wasn't the real conversation.

"How much?" Eckland asked, taking a step closer to Ian and the hat. He flexed one hand at his thigh, fisting and unfisting his fingers. His other, he rubbed across his upper lip, where more sweat had broken out.

"Five hundred," Ian said.

And Riley barely contained her gasp. Five HUNDRED dollars? For a velvet hat with bells on it? FIVE hundred? That just sounded…

"Perfect," Eckland said. "I'll take it. You can take cash?"

He was walking around with five hundred in *cash*? Before getting this job, Riley hadn't had five hundred dollars to her name. In fact, she was losing money in her back account to fees because she didn't have five hundred dollars to her name. And this guy was walking around with that much money, just in case he found this hat?

"We take cash," Ian said, but he didn't hand the hat to Eckland when Eckland reached for it. "But before I sell this, I need to make sure you're aware that it's damaged. There's a bell missing."

He held up one of the three floppy points of the hat. The other two bells jingled when he did. But the sound set Riley's teeth on edge for some reason. They were just jingle bells, and the sound shouldn't have been that much different to a sidewalk Santa ringing a bell for donations. But something… twanged against her ears in an almost painful way.

So weird. Why the hell would anyone want that hat?

The sound didn't seem to put Eckland off, though. In fact, his eyes widened, and suddenly that weird and creepy smile, the smile that stretched his face in an awkward and unnatural way, split his mouth. The same smile that had hit Riley's instincts and made her step away from him when he'd first looked at her.

Did Ian and Doreen see that smile? Did they think he looked dangerous now, too?

"I think I can find a replacement," Eckland said. He blinked and then quickly added, "My friend will probably like the flaw. Feels more authentic with a little bit missing, right." He held his hand out for the hat. "I would like to examine it, make sure it's the one I'm looking for."

"Of course."

Ian held the hat out and Eckland snatched it from him, snake fast. Or like a starving dog snapping up an offered bite of food. Riley was a little surprised Eckland didn't take Ian's fingers with that grab.

Eckland turned the hat over in his hands, studying the soft-looking material, the thick band of black and white diamonds circling the base, the three long, floppy points of padded material. Two of the three points were green, the third white. It was the white point that was missing its bell.

As he turned the hat over and looked inside, the bells jangled again, and Riley sucked in a breath, wanting to clap her hands over her ears at the discordant noise.

Doreen glanced at her, her eyes narrowed, but didn't comment. She didn't show any sign that the sound of the bells was bothering her, though. How was that possible. The sound was grating.

Riley glanced at Ian. He didn't seem bothered either. And Eckland just looked…delighted and greedy all at once.

All that hungry anticipation over a velvet hat with bells that sounded like a key scrapping over metal? She didn't get it.

When Eckland looked up, that same creepy-ass smile still stretched his mouth, looking too big for his face. His eyes were narrow, his long chin tucked back. The expression, the position of his head, left strange shadows under his eyes and in the hollows of his cheekbones, giving him a sinister appearance that made Riley want to shiver.

And then, very slowly, Eckland put on the hat.

Neither Doreen nor Ian made a move to stop him, though why they would Riley wasn't sure. She took a step forward, flexing her fingers, like she might reach for Eckland to prevent him putting on the hat. Why, though? Sure, he said he was buying it for a friend, so why would he put it on? But there was no reason for him *not* to put it on either.

Except that there was. Riley felt it in the depths of her soul. Eckland shouldn't wear that hat. *No one* should put that hat on.

A flare of light forced her eyes closed briefly. When she blinked them open again...

Eckland looked...different. The same. Still dressed in the same outfit he'd worn into the shop. But his face looked longer now. And his posture had changed, though she had trouble putting her finger on what was different. He seemed both taller and more hunched. His eyes farther apart now, which gave his entire face an even more awkwardly asymmetrical arrangement. His chin seemed pointer, too.

And his smile. His smile was a nightmare.

Yet Riley couldn't even say why. Maybe it was the faint green-blue glow in his eyes that was hard to mistake for a trick of the light now. And the way his mouth stretched wider that his face should have allowed. And his lips looked redder, like he'd put on lipstick in the brief moment her eyes had been closed. His skin was paler too, like it was powdered. And around the weird glow in his eyes, she'd swear he had… almost like a starburst painted around one eye in black and purple shadow. But faint enough she wasn't sure she was actually seeing the starburst.

Overall, though, his face just looked…different. Like a comic book Joker.

She blinked. Yeah. Like something from a comic book. All misshapen and unnaturally stretched. And the colors more extreme. That's what his face reminded her of now.

Had to be some kind of trick.

Eckland laughed, the sound as grating as the bells, and the two bells on the hat jingled again in their discordant music. Riley raised her hands to cover her ears, though she checked the movement at the last moment.

"I'd heard you two were…clever," Eckland said.

"We are." Doreen pushed her glasses up her nose again.

"That hat only has two of the three bells," Ian pointed out. Again.

Which was weird. He'd literally just told Eckland that was a flaw with the hat. He'd specifically pointed it out. Why on earth would he be repeating it but in that way like it was important information?

Everything the three said to each other didn't make sense to Riley. The words and phrases individually made sense, but the conversation as a whole didn't. She was missing something. Something important.

"Even two bells would be enough, you know," Eckland said. His head did a little jerked to one side thing and his shoulders twitched. His stance seemed crookeder and more hunched now. But he also seemed taller, so that even hunched he was looking down at everyone. Even Ian who had been objectively taller than him just a moment ago.

"No," Doreen said with a sigh. "Two bells is not enough. And you shouldn't have put that hat on."

"No one should," Ian said.

Which was exactly what Riley's instincts had insisted.

Riley looked between Eckland and the Sinclairs. What the hell was she missing?

Eckland chuckled and the sound was again a horrible scratching sort of sound that hurt Riley's ears. He tilted his head. The bells jingled.

"You're fools," Eckland said. "Fools to assume I wouldn't put it on right away. And fools to assume I wouldn't have the third bell."

He reached into his pants' pocket and pulled out a shiny, silver jingle bell. He held it between his fingers and gave it a little shake.

Riley nearly dropped to her knees the sound was so awful. How could a simple piece of rounded metal even make that sound? The noise hit her ears and made her instantly nauseous, made her want to throw up, made her eyes water and her throat tight. Her heart started to hammer. She reached out to brace herself on a nearby table when her knees wobbled.

Ian's eyes narrowed on the bell. Doreen pushed her glasses up again and straightened her shoulders.

How the hell were they not bent over double? Why wasn't the sound of those bells making them want to puke, too?

Sweat broke out along Riley's spine, across her forehead, dripped down her temples. She swiped at the dampness on her jaw with the back of her hand and shivered at the clammy wetness under her shirt. The nausea rolled through her stomach again as Eckland moved and all three bells made such a horrible noise she couldn't even describe it.

"The power," Eckland murmured. "So. Much. Power."

Power? What the hell was he talking about?

"You know," Doreen said quietly, "we've been looking for that third bell. For a long time."

Eckland smiled his truly horrible smile. And again, Riley had the impression of him being bigger, big enough he was looking down at the Sinclairs, hovering over them. His head near to scraping the store's ceiling. The top of the jester's hat did seem farther up, farther out of reach.

Why the hell would she want to reach it?

Still, her fingers flexed on the table she braced against, as if she was preparing to...leap forward? Why would she do that? She wanted to run away.

God, the noise of those bells was going to make her scream. Why wasn't anyone else reacting? She needed to get the bell in his hand away. Stop it making that noise. The other two were bad enough but when he added in that third bell... Just awful.

Yeah. That third bell. That was the one. She needed to get that one away from him.

Riley could barely think around the pain in her head now. Just knew she had to make it stop. She couldn't hear what the Sinclairs and Eckland were saying to each other anymore either. Too much noise. Discordant. Jingling. A buzzing in her ears, like insects. Like locust. Swarms of them. Descending onto the store.

This had to stop.

Driven by the need to just end the noise, Riley watched Eckland throw his head back and laugh, at least she saw the gestures of laughing. She couldn't hear anything but the awful buzzing in her head. But with his head back, he wasn't paying attention to the bell in his hand.

Hands that looked oversized and weird. But then, the bell looked larger in his hand now too. She must be imagining that. Trick of her brain because she was starting to see spots from the pain.

Ah, the pain. She had to make it stop.

She leapt forward the instant Eckland let his hand drop to his side, before he'd lowered his head. She didn't think. Couldn't think.

Jump forward and grab his wrist.

Eckland shook his arm, a gesture strong enough to pull Riley off her feet. She clung to him, too intent on the bell to notice anything else, to consider anything else. She pried at his fingers, desperate enough she drew blood as her nails scrapped over his skin.

Somewhere in the distance, she thought she heard shouting. Maybe. Under all the other noise. But she ignored it all. Her full focus on Eckland's hand, on unclenching his fingers.

The man jerked above her, his fingers spasmed. Gave her a gap to pry open two. He resisted her efforts. But the closer she got to the bell, the easier it was to think. To hear. Her brain hurt less.

Yes. She just had to get the damned thing away from him.

She pressed her nails into his wrist, hunting for that pressure point one of her roommates had tried to convince her was there, the one that would make a person's fingers jerk if you hit it right. Johnathon had never been able to make the trick work, to find the spot on anyone who actually let him try. Riley still jabbed and poked at Eckland with one hand, searching for the pressure point, desperate enough to try anything now.

His wrist was too big. Should have been able to get her

whole hand around his wrist and she couldn't. Didn't matter. She dug her fingers into his muscle and tendons, between the bones, pried at his fingers.

His skin seemed to be turning a strange green-blue color under her fingers. If she'd been able to think, she'd have wondered at that. But her only thought was the bell. And getting it out of his hand.

"No!" A roar above her. More shouts.

She could hear again. So much better. Had to finish this. Get the bell. Stop the noise completely.

She dug her fingers under Eckland's, felt metal. The bell! She scrambled and pried and pushed and managed to get her finger under the sphere of metal. Enough to snatch it forward, force it through Eckland's clenched fist.

The bell came free with a pop.

So suddenly, Riley fell backwards. She released her hold on Eckland to clutch the bell and keep it from dropping. That move meant she couldn't catch herself, and she fell into a pile of old board games. Hit the ground hard enough to steel her breath.

She looked up, trying to drag in air.

The man who had been Eckland didn't look quite human anymore. He was a pale blue-green color. His already stretched and pointed features had expanded into such an extreme exaggeration of human features they just didn't look real anymore.

And he was no longer wearing the clothes he'd had on when he walked into the store. Now he seemed to be wearing…a velvet jacket in a patchwork of alternating green, blue, and red colors. His pants were black velvet, tight to his ankles. And he wore a pair of curve-toed and tasseled black velvet shoes.

He had definitely not had those shoes on earlier.

The rest of the scene slowly sank in. Doreen hanging off the man's back. Ian scrambling at the man's arms. Doreen snatched at the hat. The bells jingled.

But this time, as Riley clutched the third bell, the sound of the other two wasn't so discordant anymore. In fact, they almost sounded…nice.

Not quite, though. There was still something off. Something wrong.

She looked down at the bell in her fist. It was round, and silver, with a line around the circumference that seemed to have a pattern etched in it. A red glowing pattern. Lines and curves almost like…words. The split opening on the bottom looked a little like a rounded cross. Inside the opening, she could just the metal sphere that created the noise when the bell shook.

The sphere looked a little odd. Like it was glowing blue-green. But she didn't have time to study it.

Above her, more shouting.

Ian yelled, "Now!"

Eckland, "No!"

And Doreen snatched the hat by one of the long points and jerked it off Eckland's head.

The sound it made when she pulled it away was a combination of sucking and tearing, and it was so gross, Riley gagged.

Eckland screamed.

A flash of bright white light.

Riley threw herself over, covering her head and eyes with her arms as a wave of heat washed over her.

CHAPTER FIVE

By the time Riley blinked the spots away, and looked around, Eckland was on the ground, collapsed to his knees.

He looked the same size as he had when he'd come into the store. The same color. Wearing his ordinary clothes. His features still awkward but the same awkward as they'd been when she'd first seen him. Not so distorted as to look unnatural.

He no longer had the hat on. And there seemed to be an injury around his head because there was a lot of dripping blood. But she didn't look close enough to see what the injury was.

Ian and Doreen were also kneeling amid the wreckage of toys that had been scattered during the fight. Ian in front of Eckland, Doreen behind. Doreen held the white and green velvet jester's hat in her hand.

Given all the blood on Eckland's head, dripping down his temples, Riley thought for sure the hat would also have blood on it. But it looked as pristine as it had when Ian brought it out.

Why was Eckland bleeding?

"Should we call someone?" she said, then had to clear her throat. She sounded like she hadn't had anything to drink in a month. She gestured at Eckland. She knew he was alive. She could see his chest rising and lowering. But all that blood…

"He'll be fine," Ian said, snarling a little as he climbed to his feet. "So long as he doesn't try to put that hat on again."

Riley wasn't so sure about Eckland being fine. But she'd absolutely love to know why taking the hat off had caused damage.

Or maybe not. Maybe it was better not to understand.

She unclenched her hand and glanced at the bell in her palm again. It looked smaller now. The etching around the circumference a swirling pattern now instead of the words she'd swear she'd seen. And the pellet inside that made it jingle wasn't glowing anymore.

Had it ever been? Had anything she'd thought she'd seen been real? Because there was no evidence that it had been. Except for Eckland' injury, he looked the same. The bell in her hand was small. The velvet hat Doreen held normal sized.

Riley looked up when Ian's shadow fell over her. He reached out a hand to help her to her feet. She wabbled a bit, so clung to him long enough to get her balance.

"What the hell happened? What was that?" she murmured, her gaze mostly on Eckland.

The man wasn't even trying to wipe the blood off his face as it dripped down his cheeks and over his eyes. That made Riley shiver.

Ian held out his hand. "Better give me the bell, Riley. It's not safe."

She glanced down at it again. Her fingers flexed around it. "It's just a bell."

"What made you grab it from Eckland?" Ian lowered his voice, but Riley didn't think Eckland was listening anyway.

"The noise. That awful sound coming from all the bells. It hurt. I thought...if I could get the loose bell away from him, it might make the horrible noise stop."

"Horrible? Not...not pleasant? It wasn't making you... You didn't want to follow Eckland? Laugh? Anything like that?"

"Laugh?" She snorted. "I wanted to barf. Someone needs to take a hammer to those bells. Bells should never make that kind of sound. Ever."

From her spot still kneeling behind Eckland, Doreen huffed out a laugh. "Wouldn't that be nice if it was as easy as smashing them with a hammer."

Ian made a sound that was half snort, half chuckle. He exchanged a look with Doreen, his eyes narrowed, then said, "Riley and I'll take the hat to the back again. You want to escort Mr. Eckland out?"

"My pleasure," Doreen said, her mouth twisted in a scowl. She took Ian's hand as he helped her back to her feet, then she passed him the hat. She glared down at Eckland. "Up," she said, her tone sharp. "This'll be the last time you try for mind manipulation power, right? All it gets you is a bleeding scalp."

"It was mine," Eckland said, snarling at the ground. "I had it in my grasp. The ability to control anyone. *Anyone*."

Doreen shook her head. "When will you people learn. We saved you from a horrible fate. Do you know what happens to people who use what's in that hat? It's a lot worse than the scars you'll have at your hairline, I can tell you that."

She hefted Eckland to his feet with surprising strength. Riley blinked. She hadn't realized Doreen was so strong. But then, Eckland looked pretty peaked and pale. Maybe he wasn't as heavy as he'd seemed like he might be earlier.

Ian gestured for Riley to follow him, so she didn't get to hear the rest of Doreen's conversation with Eckland. She did hear the bell over the front door ring, though, so she knew Doreen had gotten the man out of the shop at least. And that bell didn't do any damage to Riley's ears.

"What was that?" Riley asked Ian as he led her behind the checkout desk and to the door that went into the storage room where she never went.

She'd been in there that one time, right after being hired. She had a vague memory of that. And then her bosses had warned not to go back alone. And then…she'd never had any call to go into the back. For some reason, though, she had this feeling like she'd been to the storage room more than the one time. Huh. Strange.

It was as she remembered it. The lights were on this time, where the last, things had been dark at first. But of course, Ian had been back here when Eckland arrived, so it made sense the lights were already on. Rows of metal storage shelves stretched in front of her and off to the left and right. The space looked a lot larger than it should have been based on the size of the building. She remembered that part. She was convinced the building was actually shaped weird, like the Flatiron, more of a triangle than a square. But you couldn't really see the shape from the outside.

She'd meant to try at some point, hadn't she? Maybe she'd do that tonight on the way home.

Each of the shelves was stacked with boxes, some wooden, some glass, some plastic. There were also individual items just sitting in between some of the storage boxes. And the whole place had a strange smell to it. A little dusty maybe, but mostly it smelled like…ozone. Like the way lightning smelled. She'd never been able to put a good definition to that scent. But it did make her nose twitch.

Ian didn't lead her very far into the room this time, they went to the right about three shelves and then down that aisle about halfway, to what seemed like a perfectly random spot on one of the dozens of shelves that all looked just like this.

Where he stopped, there were three dark metal boxes, longer and rectangular, with locks on them and some etchings that reminded her of the inside of churches. She wasn't sure why. Maybe curving of the words, almost like Latin writing, but also with the shapes of certain letters that reminded her of illuminated manuscripts. The writing was pretty, even if she couldn't read it. But if she looked at it too long, the letters seemed to swirl and distort, so she blinked hard and turned away from the boxes.

With the jester's hat still in one hand, Ian dragged another dark metal box to the edge of the shelf, one that looked similar to the three smaller rectangular boxes, but large and cube-shaped instead. From the way it scraped across the lighter gray metal shelf, the box sounded heavy.

"You're ignoring my question," she said.

"Not ignoring, concentrating."

He pulled a key hung on a chain around his neck from under his shirt. The key was one of those old kinds with an ornate, almost flower shaped head, long arm, and an elaborate shaped bit at the end with the cuts to match the lock. It looked made of copper maybe, with a slight blue patina to it, but Riley couldn't be sure.

Slipping the key into the lock on the front of the box, Ian turned very gently. A slight click, and a hiss of air as the box lid lifted slightly.

Ian let out a low breath and, without looking at her, said, "Okay, hand me the bell."

Riley blinked. She'd actually forgotten she was still holding it. In fact, hadn't Ian asked for it earlier? Hadn't she already handed it to him?

She opened her palm and realized she must have misremembered those moments after Doreen had pulled the hat off Eckland because there it was, that little bell, still in the palm of her hand. It didn't look like much now. Small and cheap almost. Made of a weak sort of tin that she could crush with her fist. Nothing glowed inside. Even the etchings circling it didn't seem like a decorative pattern anymore. Just scratches.

The sort of random bit of metal that turned up at the back of junk drawers and at the bottom of storage bins.

She held her hand up, the bell in the center of her palm, offering it to Ian.

He stared at her for a long moment, then lifted the bell from her palm. She rubbed her hand against her pants, relieved to not be holding the thing anymore, even though she wasn't sure why that was a relief.

Ian wrapped his large fingers around the bell, but he was still staring at her. "You heard something bad when these bells jingled."

He wasn't exactly asking, but she still answered. "A horrible noise. Yeah. What did you hear?"

"Nothing. But I was protected from the sound." He waved at the key.

"Huh?"

"Long story, but let's just say this hat and all its bells are…better off back here than out in the world where someone like Eckland can get them all together."

"Why did you bring the hat out, then? If you weren't going to sell it to him. If it's…dangerous?"

"Dangerous. And because it was the only way to get the

third bell. The only reason he would have come looking for this—" Ian lifted the velvet jester's hat a little, "—is because he had the missing bell, and the bell told him what he needed."

"Needed for what? How could a cheap bell tell him anything?"

Ian's mouth lifted slightly. "Doesn't matter. Thanks to you, we've got all of it back now. It'll be safe here." He nudged open the lid fully and set the jester's hat inside the cube-shaped box, gently.

She looked in to see the box was lined with what looked like gold, gold covered in more of that illuminated manuscript writing and pictures Riley didn't have a chance to study. Not that her eyes wanted her to. Everything sort of swirled and melted if she stared too long. Just like the outside of the box.

There was also a little shelf inside, a small curved bit of metal tucked into the corner like a miniature floating bookshelf. On the small notch was another box, like a mini version of the larger hat box, only round instead of square.

Using the same key—which looked much too large for the job but somehow worked—Ian opened the smaller round box and tucked the third bell inside. Then he locked everything back, carefully closing lids and turning keys.

Riley swore she heard a groaning sound, a whispered cry of denial. Must be because the locks were old and resisted turning.

When Ian was finished and had pushed the box back into place on the shelf, he faced her fully. "You didn't feel the need to keep the bell? To…hold on to it?"

"The only thing I felt for that bell was the need to smash it. Why?"

"It's… It calls to people who would be inclined to…use

the power in the hat." He smiled. "Good to know you aren't one of those people. We were right to hire you."

"Huh?"

He chuckled. "Don't worry about it. Just another day at work, right?" He clapped her on the shoulder as he turned her back toward the front of the storage room and the direction out. "I was thinking of picking up some of those excellent sandwiches from the deli around the corner for lunch. You want in on that?"

"Absolutely," she said, even as her stomach growled.

"My treat. For a good day's work."

"I never turn down free food."

Ian chuckled again. "I've always liked that about you, Riley."

As they stepped back into the main shop, Riley paused to face the storage room again. A cold breeze brushed at the hair on her forehead, and she'd swear she heard something moan. But then Ian closed the door, and both the breeze and the sound cut off.

She shook her head. Must have been her imagination. Old store, old things, weird noises.

Nothing to worry about. Just another day at work.

She blinked hard a few times. Then remembered the toy section was in disarray from…something. Whatever had happened with that last customer.

"I'll go tidy up the toys," she said.

She tried to remember what had caused the mess, but she couldn't seem to recall. Probably just a customer bumping into a table. The store had so much stuff piled so close together, that sort of thing happened a lot.

"Turkey, cheese, extra mustard?" Ian said as he pulled his snazzy black bowler hat out from under the register counter and popped it onto his mass of red hair.

41

"Perfect." She gave her head another little shake, but whatever she'd just been thinking about, she'd forgotten it. Oh well. Probably wasn't important anyway.

She headed back into the labyrinth of the store to tidy the toys, looking forward to her lunch.

I JUST ATE A BUG

Now, I know what you're thinking. You're thinking I ate a bug like a cricket or something, something ordinary, that people all around the world eat, and it's just a really good source of protein. But that's not what happened at all. I didn't just eat an ordinary Earthly bug.

I ate a Bug. A Bug with a capital B.

I should probably start at the beginning, but I have to tell you, I'm not entirely sure where this story starts. I mean, maybe when the little meteorites started falling? Not the usual meteorite shower, though. At least according to the news. But at the time, I had other things to worry about, so I didn't pay that much attention. It just sounded like there were more of them than normal? Or maybe they were so small they should have been burning up in the atmosphere so everyone was surprised a lot of them were making it all the way down to the ground?

Yeah, that sounds familiar. I think that's what the talking heads had been worrying about.

So much has happened since then. Honestly, it was just a few months ago, but it feels like twenty years.

So the news had these stories, buried under political scandal headlines and the latest celebrity gossip, about an unusual meteor shower and all the tiny little rocks falling to earth when they should have burned up. And this story went by me with only minimal notice because I had just lost my job as a dog walker for a small Manhattan company, the rent was due in two weeks, and none of my fallback options— working at the local coffee shop; fast food restaurant; delivery driver—were hiring.

Losing my job wasn't my fault. I have to say that here. It wasn't my fault. I didn't know Mitsy had found and eaten a bone off the sidewalk. I always pay attention to what the dogs are doing and make sure not to let them eat street crap. I have no idea how Mitsy snuck that bone past me. The poodle is pretty smart, but still. I would have noticed her chewing on it. I swear, she picked it up sometime after I dropped her home. But I got blamed for the subsequent barffest all over the client's multimillion dollar couch. And that was my job gone.

I was considering going to a temp agency despite my fervent desire to never work in an office again. It was that bad. I mean, I would rather walk other people's dogs and clean up the strange dog's stinking poop than work in an office again. Even in New York City on a hot, muggy August day when the stench of traffic overwhelmed the smell of tree pollen that sent my allergies skyrocketing, I'd still rather be outside with the dogs. But office work was starting to look like my only option. You'd be surprised how tough some of the minimum wage jobs are to get...

Anyway, I've gotten a little off point here, haven't I?

Okay, so I was job hunting. Just minding my own business. Hoping I could cover the ConEd next month if I kept my air-conditioner turned off despite the heat. And the world erupted into mayhem. Like serious, never-thought-I'd-live-through-it chaos. An actual, honest to God, alien invasion.

And like, who thinks they'll *really* have to live through that? No one. That's why there are movies and books about alien invasions. Because we don't honestly think we'll *really* have to live through something like that.

But here we are. Smack in the middle of an alien invasion. And *of course* the aliens are Bugs. I mean, just... I would have laughed from the cliché of it all if the stupid buggers hadn't been invading my planet and causing such upheaval.

Now, here's the thing. They weren't trying to take over

the human race or anything. In fact, we weren't even of interest to them. And not because the Bugs were like viruses or bacteria or some other thing that wasn't cognizant, just going about their biology and we got in the way. Okay, well actually sort of that last part was happening. But the Bugs *knew* what they were doing. They landed on this planet on purpose. They'd built their little space crafts and headed this way because this planet had something they wanted.

And the fact that there were these hulking Earth animals called humans who thought and talked and invented stuff and had lives even if some of them didn't have jobs at the moment, none of that mattered to the Bugs. They just wanted what they wanted. Everything else on Earth be damned.

They didn't try to fight with us either. They didn't have, like, human-scorching weapons or anything. This was not the invasion pictured in science fiction. But it wasn't, like, say locus blanketing the planet either. Again, it wasn't just a species living out their biology without menace and we got in the way. The Bugs were living out their biology here, but there was menace involved too.

They invaded, literally, to destroy—and you're not going to believe this—to destroy every living cetacean on the planet. That's right. They invaded to destroy the *dolphins*.

You couldn't write this stuff.

And we couldn't exactly ask the dolphins why the Bugs hated them since we've never learned how to speak dolphin. I've heard some humans did try asking the Bugs—who *could* communicate with us, and isn't that just a we're-smarter-than-you sort of move?—but the Bugs said, "They know what they've done. Our species will conquer and survive!" And that's all they'd say about it.

So how *did* humans figure into all this as far as the Bugs were concerned? They didn't. The Bugs didn't give two flying fucks about us. We were a nuisance species, and they even told us to just stand aside while they'd destroy their sworn enemies—the *dolphins!*—and then they'd leave.

Now, you're not gonna believe this either, but a lot of assholes actually said we should *allow* this. That we should just let the aliens kill off all the dolphins and whales and leave and then get on with our lives. Can you believe that? Can you even comprehend how selfish and ignorant? I couldn't. I mean, I don't have a super high opinion of people. Okay, my opinion of the human race is pretty bad. I'm a cynic. But still. The DOLPHINS! It's like saying, yeah, let's let the aliens destroy all the pet dogs and cats and hamsters and stuff and then leave. You really just going to let aliens snuff your pet and then move on with your life?

Yeah, I know dolphins aren't pets. That's not the point. They're a part of our world and a magnificent part at that, and really, this is *our* world. If anyone's going to kill off entire species it should be us. Not that I want that. I'm just saying.

Anyway, so there was a lot of human debate all around the planet, and while the assholes were yelling at each other, the aliens went to war against the Earth's cetacean populations. And well, this just did not go over well with some of us.

A resistance formed. An actual Resistance. To fight for the lives of the dolphins (and whales—you get the point).

We armed up at first with bug spray because, well... Sentient Bugs. What do you think of first? Bug spray. But apparently space travel helped them build up a healthy natural defense against our ordinary poisons. Staying viable against all that radiation really strengthened their physiology.

So then we tried biological warfare, thinking we could give the Bugs some of our more virulent viruses. That didn't work either. We couldn't make the viruses jump species on purpose. Sure, viruses are happy to do that in their own time, but when we could really use their help, where are they? Nowhere. Just sticking to what they know best.

Next, we tried more conventional stuff like guns and flamethrowers, but I gotta tell you, bullets are useless against Bugs. They're too damned small. Even the best shot couldn't actually hit one. Plus, they move really fast and just dodged out of the way even if a bullet might have gotten close to them. And yes, we tried buckshot. That was also a nope. The pellets scattered, the Bugs dodged, ducked, and dove away, and all we got were a lot of tiny holes in the background scenery.

We finally gave up on the guns after we accidentally sank a Resistance boat. Or four.

That was the other complication. Trying to fight the Bugs out on the ocean. Humans have not built the sort of weaponry that would allow for fighting tiny insects in the ocean. We've always aimed at larger things and only killed the small stuff on accident.

Shockwaves, electromagnetic pulses, freezing, fire, various chemical agents, we tried it all. (No, we didn't try radiation. See above surviving space travel.) Nothing worked. The bloody Bugs were nearly indestructible.

And they were just slaughtering the dolphins, despite the resistance mounted by the cetacean population. We tried coordinating our efforts with the dolphins. That didn't work out so well because of the communication issues, but we tried.

And we failed. A lot.

It was getting so bad, we were starting to think we'd lose. The Bugs would destroy all cetaceans, and the assholes who said we should allow it would claim some sort of moral victory over us. But what if the Bugs did succeed? The ecosystems of all Earth oceans would be decimated. There was just no way to calculate how bad that would have been for *all* of us on this planet.

Also, what if the Bugs decided *we* were a threat? I mean, we still don't know what they have against the dolphins. We do know they're perfectly capable of mass destruction, though, so really, we couldn't just let this invasion go.

The problem was we had nothing that killed the Bugs. Or so we thought. And then, one day, purely on accident, we discovered the secret.

Stomach acid.

Human stomach acid.

Yes, the Bugs had all kinds of resistance to all kinds of other poisons and acids and things, but it turns out that the specific balance and configuration of human stomach acid is deadly to them. I'm not the biologist in the group, so I don't really get the details. I just know it works.

How we found out on accident...? Well, let's just say that poor Randal picked a hell of a time to contract a stomach flu and toss up his cookies.

So that was it. We had the answer. Except, I don't know about you, but I really hate throwing up. I just can't. I will walk over glass and dip my feet in salt and lemon juice before throwing up if I have any say in the matter at all.

But the Bugs were winning. This was a matter of life or death. We had to use this one weapon we had against them.

Turns out, I'm not the only human who isn't good at throwing up on command, though.

The answer, like the weapon itself, was discovered on accident. And I had the "honor" of making that discovery.

We were fighting with the Bugs, they were swarming, there was shouting and yelling. The seas were heaving with leaping, breeching cetaceans. There was even a giant blue whale involved in that fight, slapping at the Bugs like they were…bugs, and taking out hundreds at a time. But the little bastards just kept coming, kept rising every time they were knocked down. Nothing we did stopped them. Blood filled the seas, cetacean blood, human blood. The sounds of screaming filled the sharp, salty South Pacific air. Storm clouds built overhead, threatening a seething storm that would hamper us and not slow the Bugs down even a little bit.

I was shouting to Josephine to move the boat around because there were some big swells coming in—at that point it was impossible to tell if it was natural ocean waves or the result of so much cetacean activity, but that didn't matter. We were about to be swamped and if we didn't move quick, the boat would capsize.

I was shouting over the sounds of screaming, and splashing, and yelling, and the sharp crack of thunder too close for comfort. And I just…

Ate a Bug.

It was an accident. The little winged alien flew into my mouth, probably thrown off course by the winds, and I closed my mouth and swallowed. Reflexively. I didn't even realize what I'd done until the Bug had already gone down.

Everyone on deck froze. I froze. It felt like the world around us froze, though I was vaguely aware that the battle continued.

I kept expecting something truly awful to happen. The Bug to shoot its way out of my chest like something from a horror movie. A scratching and clawing that tore up my insides as it moved back up my esophagus to escape. My entire body to explode from some as of yet unused secret Bug weapon.

Nothing.

Nothing bad happened.

I stood there for a long moment, feeling my stomach gurgle a little as it digested my unintentional snack. Then I belched. Which was pretty gross because it tasted like nothing you'd want to taste, and I'm not going to describe how disgusting it was.

That was it. The Bug was gone.

The tiny aliens buggered off a few minutes later, leaving us bleeding and wrecked but still alive to fight another day.

And fight we will.

We have the answer now. We know what to do. We'll use this new weapon in our very next confrontation with the alien invaders. We will win this war, banishing this threat to our planet. And we'll do it with what we do best. Eat!

After, of course, we make sure I don't die from "food" poisoning.

BORED QUESTLESS

CHAPTER ONE

Kaxem ignored Rebop when he landed at the entrance to his cave in a flourish of fresh dawn air with sulfur undertones. Ignoring Rebop wasn't typically an easy feat, but Kaxem had had many years to practice. And at that moment, he had bigger things to focus on—which was saying a lot when one considered how big of a dragon Rebop was—most importantly, reorganizing his book stacks. Again. The process took a lot of concentration. Things needed to be just so. Dealing with Rebop would just have to wait.

Rebop, however, was a consummate purveyor of distraction.

"Kaxem. Hey, Kaxem."

Kaxem gently placed a book on top of a tower of volumes, frowning to make sure the stack would remain upright. The columns of books were placed around his cave in a precise way that allowed for sufficient space for his hoard and provided him maximum ability to move through the piles without knocking anything over with his tail or wings. He'd been working on the reorganization for several weeks now and was proud of the progress he'd made. Only a few more stacks to go.

"Kaxem." Rebop again. His tone more insistent, with an edge of urgency this time.

That finally caught enough of Kaxem's attention, he answered. "What?" Though he still didn't turn to face his old friend who was also sometimes the bane of his existence.

"There's a princess asleep two kingdoms over."

"Good for her." Kaxem carefully raised the next book for this column. A leather-bound masterpiece by the ancient dragon, Stanley. A real prize.

"Kaxem. A *sleeping* princess."

Since Rebop obviously expected some sort of response to his declaration on the sleeping habits of princesses, Kaxem said, "So?" absently as he flipped open the Stanley book.

"So…" Rebop drew out the word with a level of impressive incredulity. "It's a spelled sleep."

"And?"

"And we should go try to wake her up."

"What?" Kaxem turned his large head toward the blue dragon loafing around the center of his cave.

Rebop had managed to maneuver his way to that position without knocking over any of the book stacks, which Kaxem took as a triumph of his own organizational skills.

"You know," Rebop said, his large eyes whirling wider, "like in the story—with a kiss maybe."

"Why in the two worlds would we want to do that?" He shook his head and turned back to his book, tracing a talon down the table of contents. So much wisdom. He sighed. He loved this particular manuscript.

"I don't know," Rebop said. "Cause it's something to do."

"'Cause it's something to do.' Rebop, what is that

supposed to mean?" Kaxem looked up from the book again, scowling.

Rebop shrugged, a gesture that moved one wing dangerously close to a pile of Kaxem's books. Then flopped down on the cave floor, onto one of the many jewel-toned rugs scattered between book stacks. "Do you have anything else to do?"

Kaxem rolled his eyes and turned his back to the lolling dragon. "A lot actually, yes."

Did he have anything else to do? He had all these books to reorganize. Again. After his last acquisition a few weeks ago, he'd had to rethink his entire system. No matter that he'd just reorganized everything right before that. One could never reorganize one's books too often.

Shaking his head, he placed the Stanley on the top of its new home stack and picked up another book from a pile that still needed to be sorted.

"So shall we go, Red?" Rebop poked at Kaxem's wing impatiently when Kaxem made the mistake of passing too close.

"Stop that." He slapped Rebop's talon away. "And don't call me Red. Where are we going?"

"To Polsidia. The princess. Remember?"

Kaxem looked up from the spell book he'd opened. Crinkling his thick brow ridges as he tried to understand what Rebop was on about. "Explain to me again why we would want to wake up this princess?"

"Well... Maybe there's a reward."

"We don't need a reward." Both their current hoards were sufficient. Kaxem's book hoard was the most impressive in the entire valley.

Although. Didn't princesses sometimes have libraries?

"Polsidia, you say." Which royal families were in

Polsidia? "What does the princess look like?" He didn't keep up on royalty much, but maybe a description would help him pinpoint the family in question, which would tell him if the quest—and the potential library—were worth the effort.

"I don't know for sure. I mean I've never seen her, but I've heard she's around so high—" Rebop held up his hand a bit over five foot above the cave floor, "—blond hair, pale skin, blue eyes…"

Kaxem held up a taloned-tipped finger. "Wait a minute, you mean she's an elf?"

"No," Rebop said through the side of his mouth. His large purple eyes danced away from Kaxem's gaze.

"Wrong coloring for a fairy," Kaxem murmured, lowering his brow ridges as he frowned. Fairies in this part of the world were typically browner and ordinarily had some shade of gold or green eyes. And a lot of them didn't have hair, blond or otherwise. "Is she a pixie?"

"No." Rebop's attention turned to the valley outside the wide cave entrance as he casually twirled one finger in a vague gesture. "She's a human."

"Human!" Kaxem dropped his book with a thud that echoed off the black crystalline walls. "Are you serious? Wake up a human? *Kiss* a human? Do you know what kind of germs it could have? Yuck. Besides, what would you even *do* with a human princess once you woke her up? Provided you could wake her up in the first place."

Rebop scratched absently at a loose blue scale. "What was the first question?"

"Are you serious?"

"Well… Maybe she's a dragon bespelled by an evil witch —like that frog prince in Dovenshire, remember—and a kiss will turn her back into a dragon."

Kaxem's scowl deepened. "I thought the kiss was supposed to wake her up."

"That too." Rebop picked up the forgotten spell book and placed it randomly on the top of an already perilously tall stack.

Kaxem was too distracted to pay attention. He could reorganize it later. "A bespelled dragon as a *human*?"

Rebop ignored him and plucked a book from the middle of a stack that Kaxem only barely kept from toppling. "Can I borrow this one?"

"Sure." Kaxem re-balanced the stack. "Now could you please explain to me why anyone would turn a dragon into a human, then put her to sleep?"

"Maybe an evil witch turned her into a human. Then her fairy godmother put her to sleep so she wouldn't have to suffer the torture of being human."

"That's absurd." Though not having to suffer the torture of being a human made a kind of sense. "Where did you hear about all this, anyway?"

Rebop scratched the top of his head, carefully removing several loose blue scales. "I heard it from Tarsina, who heard it directly from Melina, who's just returned from Polsidia."

"Melina! Melina is old and crazy!"

"Just because her horn curves at the end, doesn't mean she's crazy. Your horns curve in, Red, and that doesn't make you crazy."

"I'm not a unicorn. And don't call me Red. You know perfectly well my scales are burnt sienna, not red. Furthermore, I'm not flying half the day to wake up a human-maybe-dragon princess that may or may not be there because Tarlina heard a story from a crazy unicorn."

"It was Tarsina, not Tarlina."

"I don't care! I'm not going. I have too much to do here."

Kaxem turned abruptly, knocking over two stacks of books with his tail, and walked out to the ledge in front of his cave.

Rebop followed close behind, scratching his head with the spiked tip of his tail. "She might have a library." He took up a perch next to Kaxem on the ledge and began scratching the scales on his forearm.

"Are you shedding again?" Kaxem asked without looking at him.

"Yes. So what do you think?"

"I think humans never have really good libraries. They're always missing the most important books in the realms."

Kaxem extended his wings, soaking up the early rays of the sun. A shadow inched over the green valley below, slowly making way for the morning light. The dawn air was fresh and scented with cold water and a loamy flavor that spoke of home. A few dragons sat on cave ledges around the valley, also taking in the rising sunrays. Several others were already at the stream that wound through the base of the valley, wading in for their morning baths.

"Come on," Rebop pleaded. "I'm so bored. Just this one last quest. Please!"

Kaxem sighed. "Oh, don't beg, Rebop."

Really, he'd get no peace if he tried to resist. Rebop was surprisingly stubborn about some things. The newest book reorganization would just have to wait. And if the human princess *did* unexpectedly have a passable library with some good books, well, he'd just have to reorganize everything again anyway.

"All right!" He let out a huff that spread a stream of smoke onto the morning air. "I'll go. But I'll be willing to bet we don't find anything."

Rebop grinned a grin only a fellow dragon could

appreciate, and launched himself into the sky, leaving a pile of blue scales behind.

Kaxem outwardly resigned himself to the situation with a sigh, then more enthusiastically than he wanted to admit, jumped off the ledge and caught a thermal upward to join his hovering friend.

CHAPTER TWO

"Would you look at that line." Kaxem whistled.

"I told you there was something going on." Rebop pumped his wings once in triumph.

Below the circling dragons, rose a multi-turreted castle on a hill surrounded by a thick forest of pine trees. Noonday sunlight sparkled on the castle's white stone walls. Bright yellow flags snapped and sputtered from the highest spires.

And from the main gate, across the drawbridge, down and around the hill, and into the forest, stretched a line of creatures ranging from the lowliest gnome to the highest ranking elf, from shining knights to common farmers, from ogres and trolls to fairies and pixies.

Each awaiting their chance to wake the princess.

"Rebop." Kaxem looked skeptically at the crowd. "That line is not moving. We could be here for a month."

"In all honesty, I thought there'd be a weeding out process. You know. Like a challenge of some sort. Then, only the ones who passed had a chance to wake up the princess."

"Maybe we had better ask one of those people. Perhaps there is a challenge and these are the ones that passed."

"Awfully easy challenge, then," Rebop mumbled as they began their descent.

"Pardon me." Rebop tapped the leprechaun on the shoulder.

"What?" The leprechaun turned, looked up, and took two steps backward, letting out a high-pitched screech. "Well!" he huffed indignantly, straightening his red cap. "And what would you be doing here, you giant lizard?"

"No need to be rude." Rebop bristled, the spikes along his spine rising and falling in an irritated wave.

Kaxem had never been very fond of leprechauns either. But they did need answers, and the leprechaun was the last one in line.

The leprechaun pointed a finger at Rebop. "You should have announced yer mass before sneaking up on a person like that."

"Mass! What do you mean calling me Mass?"

Kaxem placed a restraining claw on his friend's forearm. "He just meant your size."

"So what brings yer kind to this event?" The leprechaun continued to glare at Rebop while he straightened his green tunic and made a show of brushing dirt from his sleeve.

"Is this the line to wake up the princess?" Kaxem asked, trying a smile to get them back on track. The smile only started the leprechaun shuddering. Kaxem let the expression drop. Dragon smiles were an acquired taste.

"Aye, yer in the right line," the leprechaun said, staring up at them from the side of his eyes. "And at the right end I might add. Pretty quick for dragons, aren't you?"

Kaxem took a calming breath.

Rebop returned the leprechaun's glare, his brow ridges coming down low over his whirling purple eyes. "I don't like the little fellow much, Kaxem. What say I step on him. Then we'd be one up in line."

The leprechaun blanched, took another step backward and bumped into the troll standing behind him.

"Watch it, dwarf," the troll growled, then turned forward again to continue his quiet waiting.

The leprechaun stepped away from the troll, wisely not pointing out the troll's mistake. Looking back at the dragons, he caught their toothy smiles and huffed to himself in quiet, offended mumbles. Then turned his back on them and faced the back of the troll's over-large thigh.

"I've never met such a rude leprechaun," Rebop said, a statement that was blatantly untrue. "Do you think he could have passed the test to get in to see the princess?"

"I don't know. Maybe this line leads to the test, then from there those who pass go on to see the princess?"

"Awfully complicated," Rebop said.

"Or maybe the line is the test," a new voice said.

Rebop and Kaxem both turned to see a human woman who had walked up behind them unnoticed. Her long red hair hung in two plaits, one over each shoulder of her green leather tunic, and her pale skin looked a little greenish in the dabbled sunlight spilling down through the trees.

"Now there's an interesting notion." Kaxem scratched his jaw. "I've never read of anything like that before." A line as a test? Fascinating idea.

"Just a thought." The red-haired human shrugged. "I don't really know for sure one way or the other. By the way, my name is Gretta."

"I'm Kaxem, and this is my friend Rebop."

"Rebop." The human frowned. "That's a strange name for a dragon."

"I was named after my mother's grandfather," Rebop answered pleasantly.

"Well, it's nice to meet you both," Gretta said with a crooked smile.

Kaxem frowned at Rebop, who he'd known for almost a century now. "I never knew you were named after your great-grandfather. I just thought your mother was a little weird."

"Oh, no. She was just very fond of her grandfather. Gretta, what brings you to this line? Are you going to try waking up the princess?"

"Actually, I'm just a sort of pack mule. I've brought a prospective with me from over the mountains." She turned to show the black leather backpack she wore.

"What do you have in there, some sort of trick to wake the princess?" Rebop poked the pack with one sharp talon.

"Watch that poking!" a muffled shout came from inside the pack, and a small head appeared over the top. The little man had long brown hair and a brown beard that disappeared down into the pack, with dark brown eyes in the middle of a brown face. He scowled up at the blue-scaled face that loomed over him. "Do you mind?"

"What in the two worlds is that?" Rebop asked Gretta.

"I can very well answer for myself. I am Drekel O'Gram, dwarf of the Octimom Mount."

"He's going to try waking up the princess," Gretta supplied.

"You are exceptionally good at stating the obvious." Drekel huffed, the grunt making his mustache bounce.

"Seems a bit small for a dwarf," Rebop said.

Kaxem was more interested in the whys. "Why on the two worlds would a dwarf want to wake up a human princess?"

"Same reason as all the rest of you grubbers," the dwarf shouted. "The reward! Gold beyond even a dwarf's dreams."

"That's a lot of gold," Rebop said, helpfully.

Drekel glared at him. "And all of my people are this size. In fact, I'm tall among my clan."

"Are you sure about this reward?" Kaxem asked.

"Of course, you giant tomato. Why else would anyone travel all the way to Polsidia to wake up a human?"

"I am not red," Kaxem said primly. "I'm burnt sienna."

"You're a fool like the rest of these grubbers. None of you stand a chance of wakin' that girl," Drekel shouted.

Those hopefuls within hearing range grumbled rude replies, then returned to their silent vigil.

"Do you know the secret to waking her up?" Rebop asked with genuine interest.

"Don't pay too much attention to him," Gretta said pleasantly. "He talks big, but he doesn't know any more than the rest."

"Gretta. Would you kindly keep your overworked mouth shut!" Drekel snarled.

"Oh hush up, you old grouch. I may have to carry you around, but I don't have to put up with your ego or your surly temperament."

"Humph!" Drekel grunted, turning his back as best he could on Gretta and the two dragons.

Gretta smiled.

Rebop asked the obvious question. "Why do you have to carry a dwarf around?"

"Lost a bet." She shrugged. "Do you have any ideas about waking up the princess?"

"I thought maybe a kiss would work."

Kaxem shivered at the thought. Such a gross idea. The *germs*!

"Possibly," Gretta said, nodding thoughtfully. "But wouldn't you need lips?" She looked pointedly at the two dragons' large, teeth-filled, lipless mouths.

Kaxem and Rebop looked at each other, then back at the human.

"I forgot about lips," Rebop said.

"That's okay," Gretta said. "I mean, everyone has probably already thought about a kiss anyway. Everything nowadays is cured with a kiss. I can't imagine this line would still be this long if all it took was a kiss to wake her."

"Maybe the kiss has to come from someone specific," Kaxem piped in. The circumstances were not much to his liking, but he could never resist a theoretical discussion.

"Maybe the answer's in this book," Rebop said, presenting a book for the group to see.

"*102 Ways to Wake Up a Sleep Spelled Princess*," Gretta read the title. "Bit on the nose. But I like it."

"Where'd you get that?" Kaxem gaped at his friend.

"From your stacks. It's the book I asked to borrow. Remember?"

"Oh, yes, of course. I'd forgotten about that." He frowned, his brow ridges drawing down deeply enough, his eyes narrowed. "You know, I didn't realize I had a book titled *102 Ways to Wake Up a Sleep Spelled Princess*." He prided himself on keeping track of his hoard, but honestly, at this stage, things did slip through. That's why he needed to reorganize everything every once in a while. Looked like it was time for a newer categorization system.

"Maybe you should start keeping a list of all the books you have," Rebop offered helpfully.

Kaxem scowled. He did keep a list. In his head. His scowl softened. Actually, a written list did sound like a good idea. It might take time, but he'd have an even *better* system for organizing his books then.

"I'll consider that when we get home," he said. "In the meantime, I say we look over the hundred and two ways to wake up a princess and see if one applies to our situation."

"But how do we know which will apply to our situation, when we're not exactly sure what 'our' situation is?" Gretta wrinkled her brow and curled one side of her mouth up.

"You're right, of course," Kaxem said, a little embarrassed a human had had to point that out. Good thing dragons didn't blush. He straightened his shoulders and fluttered his wings a little to make himself look larger and more important. "First, we must assess exactly what our situation is. Now, what facts do we have?"

"Well, we know there's a princess," Rebop said.

"And we know she's asleep," Gretta added.

"Brilliant!" Drekel exclaimed from the depths of the black backpack. "With so much intellect at work, you'll have the problem solved any minute now."

Everyone ignored the dwarf.

"We're also pretty sure she's a human princess," Kaxem continued. "That should narrow things a bit. How is the book arranged, Rebop?"

"There are individual sections, but they're divided by spellcasters not castees. We have to know *who* put the princess to sleep."

"That's easy." Gretta brightened. "Don't you fellas keep up with your history. The Polsidian royal family of Manicno has been plagued by the same evil witch for the past two centuries. Every couple of decades or so, someone in the royal family manages to insult her, and she doles out some spell or other as punishment. One story claims she sent thousands of warty toads to overrun the castle." Gretta shuddered. At Rebop's wide-eye, silent question, she said, "I do not like toads."

"You're sure the spellcaster is an evil witch and not a fairy or sprite or something, right?" Kaxem asked.

"Positive. She's definitely an evil witch."

"Let me see." Rebop ran his talon down the books table of content. "Evil witch, evil witch... Ah! Here we are. Evil Witch. So we have: Poisoned Apple, Pricked Finger, Scented Rose...," Rebop read the subsections.

"Too bad there's not a general spell for waking a human sleep-spelled princess," Kaxem said.

"'General Spell for Waking a Human Sleep-Spelled Princess'," Rebop read.

"Marvelous." And surprisingly convenient. "That makes this a lot simpler."

"Page two hundred and sixty-four." Rebop began flipping pages.

"Page two hundred and sixty-four," Gretta exclaimed. "But there are only a hundred and two spells in that book. Why so many pages?"

"Oh, well, there's a lot of background information." Rebop angled the book for Gretta. "See, this chapter begins with a short description of 'Evil Witch,' then goes on to discuss possible motivations, psychology, variations, mistakes, etc."

"Each spell may take up more than one page also," Kaxem added. He simply loved spells. Spell books were one of his favorites for adding to his hoard.

"So what does the 'General Spell for Waking a Human Sleep-Spelled Princess' have to say?" Gretta asked.

"Yes, how does it work?" Drekel said, twisting around in the backpack to look over Gretta's shoulder, suddenly very interested.

"Hold on, now." Rebop pulled the book back against his massive, blue-scaled chest. "Why should we share this with you, dwarf? I mean if there is a reward, you might try to cheat us out of it."

"The book is mine, after all." Kaxem took a half step toward the dwarf.

"Now just hold on." Drekel held up his little hands to ward off the glares of the two dragons. "What would you two say to a deal? We could share what's in the book and then split the reward."

"And why would we want to do that? The book is ours. We could have the whole reward." Rebop smiled at his own cunning.

Kaxem gave him a little pat on the back above his wings in encouragement.

"Yes," the dwarf said, "but then you'd be waiting in this line all day and probably well into tomorrow." Drekel grinned and paused for effect. "But I have a way for all of us to get to the front of this line in a snap."

CHAPTER THREE

Kaxem and Rebop exchanged a long look. For his part, Kaxem didn't want to wait in this line into tomorrow. He was okay with indulging Rebop for a day, but two was pushing his tolerance. Especially without the promise of a *really* good library on the other side.

In unison, Kaxem and Rebop both glanced back at the long line of various creatures patiently waiting to reach the castle. Birds chirped in the surrounding forest. A gentle breeze brushed Kaxem's scales. It was a lovely day.

And the line hadn't moved since they'd arrived. Not even a single step.

He and Rebop exchanged another long look.

Then Rebop said, "That doesn't sound fair to the rest of these folks who've been waiting in line for what I can only assume has been a long time."

Rebop had a streak of fairness that was a league long. It was one of his more endearing qualities, Kaxem had to admit.

"How do we know the line's not just an illusion?" the dwarf asked through a knowing grin, his bushy brown eyebrows disappearing up into his hair line.

Oh. Well. Kaxem hadn't considered that. He glanced back at the unmoving line again. The rude leprechaun had *seemed* real enough. But that didn't mean he wasn't an illusion.

"The challenge," Gretta whispered.

"Can you tell if the line is an illusion before you move us to the front?" Kaxem asked, his attention on the winding stream of creatures. He could just remember reading something on this topic very recently.

"That's all part of it, dragon," Drekel shouted, bouncing in the backpack.

Gretta swatted at him, grunting as the motion jostled her.

"I don't understand." Rebop scratched blue scales from his jaw.

"Simply put, in deference to a dragon, the spell I have will only move us to the front of the line if the line is an illusion. Otherwise, nothing happens."

Rebop frowned at Kaxem. "What do you think?"

Kaxem frowned at the dwarf, meeting his smug gaze. He didn't like to admit it but, "I think I believe the dwarf, Rebop."

Drekel's smile actually managed to get bigger, spreading his beard wide and revealing a straight row of very white teeth.

"But I don't trust him."

Drekel's smile turned down.

"You're right not to trust my obnoxious little burden here," Gretta said. "But for a deal to be struck you must try to trust each other a little bit. Otherwise, we're at an impasse. If you dragons give the spell first, Drekel could move only himself and wake up the princess before you could catch him. But if Drekel moves us first, you could still refuse him the spell."

"Thank you for that insightful analysis, Gretta," Drekel said dryly.

Everyone ignored him.

"I have an idea," Rebop said. "What if we gave Drekel most of the spell, all but the last line, then he moves us all, then we go to the princess together and finish the spell together."

"You're requiring that I trust you overgrown lizards quite a lot," Drekel huffed. "What good does half a spell do me? You could still refuse me the rest once we move."

"If we give our word of honor..." Kaxem began.

"Bah!" Drekel shouted.

"If we left out only two words?" Rebop ventured.

"Ah! Now that I might be willing to go along with." Drekel tugged at his beard. "Only so many words, right. Shouldn't be too hard to guess..."

"Is it a deal, then?" Gretta asked.

Both dragons and dwarf nodded in unison.

"Let me read the spell," Kaxem said, motioning to Rebop for the book. "I'll know which two words to leave out."

Rebop handed him the book with one long talon holding it open to the correct page.

Kaxem cleared his throat, skimmed the spell, then read aloud. "Through trails and tricks I've come, this princess to wake. With magical words, her eyes will I open. Levan nock tura newara (blank) pake. Tu ora lo (blank) emena havake."

"You read that wonderfully, Kaxem," Rebop said.

"Thank you, Rebop."

"Well, you picked two perfect words, dragon," Drekel grumbled, but with an edge of appreciation. "That spell will fall flat if the wrong ones are used."

"If the right combinations of wrong words are used, that spell could be dangerous," Gretta commented.

"Your turn, dwarf," Kaxem said.

"All right, then. Let me down, girl," Drekel ordered.

With his feet finally on the ground, the dwarf began to chant low and in a strange tongue. Kaxem prided himself on his skills with languages and even he'd never heard this language before. He leaned in a little closer, trying to pick out a familiar word or syntax. But the meaning eluded him.

When Drekel finished his chant, the dragons looked up...

To discover they were standing at the foot of the drawbridge to the castle.

The line had disappeared.

"That was very good," Rebop said to the dwarf.

"I was expecting a sensation of some sort," Kaxem said, "but I didn't feel a thing." He quickly tried to remember the dwarf's spell, but there'd been too much mumbling. And all in a language he didn't know. Which was annoying.

"Shall we go find the princess?" Gretta gestured toward the castle's open portcullis.

They walked over the drawbridge, through the gates and into the castle courtyard. All around them were sparkling white walls and elegant drapes of greenery. A central fountain in the courtyard was topped with twin cherubs spitting clean water into the pool below. Kaxem thought he picked up a faint scent of something minerally in the water, but nothing like poison. Or sleeping potions. So it was probably okay to drink.

One thing that seemed to be missing, however, were other humans. The courtyard, the battlements, the gated horse stables to one side, all empty of humans—and horses for that matter.

"Where do you suppose she is?" Rebop whispered.

"I don't know." Kaxem glanced up at the multi-story

central keep. Even for a dragon, it looked quite tall. "It's awfully big, isn't it."

Big but with human proportions worked into the architecture. Which meant difficult navigation for a searching dragon.

Which was probably the point, though, wasn't it?

"I would guess she's in the top room of the tower," Gretta suggested quietly, pointing to the castle's central tower. Sunlight glinted off its pointed red-tiled roof.

"That's quite a climb," Rebop whispered. "Do you suppose we'll fit in that room?" He glanced at Kaxem.

Kaxem assessed the tower in question. "Oh, I should think so," he whispered back. "That's a pretty large tower."

"And I'm sure they've made allowances for dragons," Gretta whispered.

"Why are you fools whispering!" Drekel bellowed.

A flock of previously unsee ravens cawed and took to the air in a flurry of black feathers and bird poop.

"Shhhh," Rebop chided the dwarf. "The princess is sleeping."

"I know she's sleeping, you giant blue frimpet. That's why we're here. *To wake her up!*"

"Oh. Yes. Sorry." Rebop shrugged and a single blue scale fluttered to the ground. He scratched his forearm.

"Drekel, can that spell of yours get us into that room?" Kaxem asked, his gaze still on the window at the top of the tallest tower.

"Nope. Won't work like that."

"Can't you dragons fly us all up to the window?" Gretta asked.

Kaxem nodded. "And I think we can fit through that window. But lifting off from the courtyard will be hard."

The courtyard didn't have quite enough space for two

dragons with fully extended wings, and there was very little by way of breeze inside the enclosed area to help. Technically, Kaxem supposed they could get airborne from inside the courtyard, but it would prove pretty taxing.

"Right, then," Rebop said. "Back out over the drawbridge."

The small group followed Rebop to a clearing just the other side of the bridge, the sound of their passage along the wooden treads echoing after them. The murky water filling the mote moved sluggishly past, and Kaxem was certain he saw a few of those large fish with the sharp teeth in the dark depths. At least if he and Rebop needed a snack, there was one on hand.

In the clearing, Gretta helped Drekel back into the black leather backpack, then Rebop gave them both a gentle boost up to Kaxem's neck.

"Hold tight now," Kaxem warned. "Lift off can be a bit jerky."

The two dragons pumped their powerful wings and took to the air with only a single squeak of protest from Drekel.

They circled once to fix the position of the tower window and to make sure it actually was big enough for them. It was. Quite large actually. Nearly a floor to ceiling hole in wall of the very top floor of the tower. It actually reminded Kaxem of a dragon's cave entrance more than something a human princess might have in her tower. But maybe human architecture had advanced in recent years.

They glided through the window and came to an abrupt stop inside the tower's top room. The large chamber was empty but for a small bed against the wall opposite the window. On the bed slept a small, blond, human girl. She wore a pale pink, ankle length nightgown, a color that was a remarkable match to her pale pink skin.

"She's sort of pretty for a human," Rebop commented as he helped Gretta and Drekel off of Kaxem's neck.

"Bah! She's human," Drekel said. "They're all pretty ugly."

Gretta set the backpack down and let the dwarf out again.

"Gretta's human, though, and she's not ugly," Rebop said.

Drekel snorted.

Gretta shrugged and said, "I'm not really human. It's actually quite a long story. I'll tell you all about it sometime."

"I'll look forward to it," Rebop said. "I like long stories."

"Yes, he does," Kaxem said, whose own curiosity was also peaked.

The group crept quietly to the princess's bed. "Who should recite the spell?" Drekel asked, finally giving in to the whispering.

"I say we let Kaxem," Rebop said, quietly. "He read it so beautifully the first time."

"Thank you, Rebop. Drekel, do you agree that I read the spell?"

"Now, we're all of the same mind here, right? We are all to split the reward if we wake her?" Drekel looked at the other three closely, his little eyes narrowed so much they were hard to see around his shaggy hair and full beard.

"Of course," Kaxem agreed.

"Fine then, dragon. Read away."

"Rebop, does the spell require any preparation or set up? Any special hand gestures?" Kaxem asked. Spells could be very specific. Even general-use ones. Kaxem didn't want to risk accidentally blowing up the castle before he'd discovered if there was a library with useful books here.

Rebop opened the book, scanned the introductory passage. "Nothing's mentioned. Just says it has to be recited in the presence of the princess."

"Well then, hand me the book, and we'll get this little adventure over with at last." Kaxem looked at the spell, then raised his head and solemnly recited the complete passage to the sleeping human. "Through trails and tricks I've come, this princess to wake. With magical words, her eyes will I open. Levan nock tura newara meck pake. Tu ora lo hotra emena havake."

"Has it worked?" Drekel crowded close to the princess's bed and stood on his toes to see the girl's face. "Is she waking up?"

All four watched breathless as first the princess's eyes fluttered then opened. She blinked several times, turned to look at her saviors, and said, "You've come! I knew I could get all of you together."

Kaxem frowned and glanced at Repob, who frowned at Gretta, who raised her brows at Drekel, who was busy scowling at the princess.

Gretta was the first to recover. "You mean you were expecting us the whole time?" she asked.

"Well, not you specifically," the girl said. She had a bouncy, happy voice in a pleasant register that didn't hurt Kaxem's ears. That was a bonus. "The diviner was only able to predict that there should be two dragons, a dwarf, and a pixie."

"Pixie!" Kaxem and Rebop exclaimed in unison.

"I told you I wasn't really human." Gretta shrugged.

"That was part of the problem," the princess said. "I was sure that I could get two dragons and a dwarf to cooperate given the proper circumstances, but I was very worried about a pixie getting involved. Especially with a dwarf."

"Hazards of gambling," Gretta said through a crooked smile.

"As it stands, you four did find each other and managed

to cooperate enough to get here and awaken me. That was no small feat. Fegil will be so pleased."

"Hold on a bloomin' minute," Drekel shouted, throwing his short arms into the air. "Is there a reward or not? Who's this Fegil? Why a dwarf, two dragons, and a pixie? What the blazes is going on here, princess?"

"Fegil is the diviner who foresaw your coming. But the sleeping princess part was my idea. Say, how long was I asleep anyway?"

"About three weeks," Rebop provided.

"That's all? Well, I could swear it was longer. Anyway…"

"I still don't get it," Drekel complained.

"It's simple, sir. You ask of a reward? Your reward is to receive your hearts' desire. Adventure."

"Adventure?" all four said at once.

"My heart's desire is gold," Drekel said under his breath.

"Adventure, friends," the princess said, clapping her hands together. "Each of you has been craving adventure for most of your lives. My kingdom requires the help of brave individuals like yourselves. Fegil looked to the spirit world to find our hope and saw you four. And now you are here at last, despite all misgivings, and you've proven yourselves more than worthy of the tasks that lie ahead. Destiny guides us. You four have been chosen by fate to accompany me into history. From this day on you will live the lives you have always craved. Get ready, my new friends, for you are about to begin the greatest adventures of your life times!" She raised her thin arms into the air, her fists punching toward the roof.

The stunned silence following this speech lasted for a full minute.

Then Drekel said, "I'd rather have the gold."

"Yeah," Rebop said, scratching at a loose scale. "I think I'd rather just have the gold, too."

"I'd prefer books, being completely honest," Kaxem said. "Do you have a decent library around here?"

"What do you mean?" the princess asked, tiny mouth agape. She fluttered pale lashes over blue eyes too large for her face. "There is no gold. Or...books. You're supposed to want adventure."

Kaxem looked at Rebop and raised his brow ridges.

Rebop shrugged, then looked back at the princess. "Sorry, princess, but I don't think we'll take the adventure."

"Are you sure there's no gold?" Drekel pleaded.

"What gold?" the princess snapped, some of the dulcet, pleasant pitch of her voice dropping away.

"Rude," Gretta commented dryly.

"We'd better be going," Kaxem said to Rebop, nodding toward the window, inching away from the bed. Even if there was a library somewhere in this castle, he was certain now it wouldn't have any good books in it.

The princess threw her legs over the edge of the high mattress, looking frantically at her four would-be heroes.

"It was very nice to meet you, princess," Rebop said.

Gretta helped Drekel back into the leather backpack, mumbling, "I've got to give up gambling with dwarves."

Rebop once again helped them both onto Kaxem's neck.

The princess, now on her slippered-feet, frantically waved her arms and yelled, "Wait! Wait!"

Everyone ignored her.

As the two dragons leapt from the tower window, Kaxem said, "Rebop, why was your great-grandfather named Rebop?"

"He wasn't," Rebop said. "He was named Bop."

TING LING

CHAPTER ONE

Where the hell was that bell sound coming from? Albert shook his head hard, but that didn't help. No, the sounds weren't in his head. They were around here somewhere. But where?

Albert hunted behind the large, comfortable couch and found only a few hairballs and a stray Cheeto. No bells.

He looked under the side chairs flanking his coffee table. Both were big heavy Lazy-boy chairs. Nothing under either one except some lint and another couple of Cheetos. Damn Cheetos got everywhere. When had he last eaten Cheetos? A week ago? More? Probably ought to move the furniture around and vacuum underneath more.

Once he figured out where that fucking bell sound was coming from.

He checked behind the TV stand, found nothing but dust, the inch of space behind the bookshelves where they didn't quite sit over the baseboard properly. Nothing again. Not that he expected anything there. But by that stage he'd checked every other nook and cranny in his apartment and…nothing.

He heard the bells in every room, but stronger in the

living room-kitchen area of the one-bedroom apartment. The place was arranged weirdly so there was also a nook off the kitchen he used for an office. The bells weren't so loud there. No. The sound was definitely louder in the open living room. But he'd checked every possible place they could be coming from.

Hands on hips in the middle of the living room, he turned in a circle. In the walls maybe?

Shit. That would be bad. And weird. How the hell was he going to get into the walls without releasing a bunch of mice and cockroaches onto his apartment? This was New York City. Even with the best maintenance and exterminator practices, there were mice and roaches in the walls. It was a fact of life. The only way to keep them out of your apartment was to keep all the possible ways in sealed off. No holes. Anywhere. He'd learned that the hard way when a hole behind the mini-fridge in his office near the baseboard had been letting in a steady stream of mice for about a month before he figured out where the hell they were getting in.

That month still lived in his memory as a little slice of hell on earth. No more. No more holes.

But the bells were going to drive him nuts if he couldn't make them stop. A constant ting-a-ling-a-ling. Ting-a-ling-a-ling. Over and over. A break, randomly. Then more ringing. He'd hunted outside, opening the windows despite the cold to check and see if a bird had built a nest anywhere on the brick walls or over someone's currently dormant windowsill air conditioner. No birds. No stray nests. No random bells somehow caught on the red bricks.

Had to be the walls. But he was no way in hell going to punch holes in the walls and let the mice in again.

He supposed he could always move.

Albert shook himself hard at the thought. No one would buy this place with a constant bell sound anyway.

Maybe if he could pinpoint the exact spot, he could get the super up here to help open the wall and then get it closed again before the mice were any the wiser. So long as the hole got sealed up quickly, he should be good.

He definitely couldn't sleep another night with those bells. One was enough. And sleep wasn't exactly how he'd define his night. Noise cancelling headphones were tough to sleep in and didn't block all the sound anyway.

Ting-a-ling-a-ling. Ting-a-ling-a-ling.

For a brief moment, he worried someone or something like a cat had gotten caught in the walls. Or a kid? Shit. That would be horrible. And him not realizing it for a full twenty-four hours!

But the bells were too consistent. They did stop randomly. But a kid or even a cat would get tired and stop for longer than a minute after all this time. Right?

Albert walked along the wall in his living room, trying to pinpoint the sound. The hiss of his heaters coming on complicated things. Oh, he could still hear the bells alright, but pinpointing the source over the sounds of hissing and clanking from the heaters proved difficult. He finally had to stop for a few minutes, until the heat was going and the noise of it coming on stopped.

One thing he'd give his apartment building, they didn't stint on the heating. At least not by February. God help them if it got cold in October. Saving oil. No heat despite the dip to below the temperature tipping point that was supposed to turn the heat on automatically—Albert thought the building manager made sure that tipping point temperature thing was adjusted lower for October just to save money. But by the middle of winter, the heat was always in full swing.

Sometimes too much heat. He had to crack his windows to balance it out. But that was fine. He preferred being hot to being cold anyway.

Once the heat settled, he went back to trying to pinpoint the exact location of the bell sound. Ting-a-ling-a-ling. Ting-a-ling-a-ling. God that was going to drive him nuts.

He really hoped it wasn't coming from someone trapped in the walls. How would they even get in there, though. There wasn't any work being done on the building at the moment. No way into the walls unless you were dumb enough to open the walls yourself and risk a mice invasion for…reasons.

Albert couldn't think of a single reason.

His cellphone rang from its place charging near the couch. He ignored it. That was his work phone and he was on his lunch break. He didn't take work calls on his lunch break.

Damn it. Where were those bells?

He followed the weird curve in his apartment that led toward the kitchen, past his two windows that actually had a view of a patch of green park and not a view of one of the neighboring buildings. The patch of green was a cemetery, but still. It was a beautiful one with lovely old tombs and lots of grass and trees. Made him feel very Victorian to go for his daily walks there.

The bells seemed to be coming from an area closer to the corner of the apartment, at the edge of the kitchen. Not a wall shared with a neighbor. He'd already asked both his immediate next-door neighbors if the bells were theirs anyway. And gotten some strange looks from the old woman in 14H and a polite no from the middle-aged man in 14K. He didn't know his neighbors' names, just knew them well enough to say hello, talk about the weather if they were riding in the elevator together, maybe bring them their mail if some got into his box on accident. It wasn't that he wasn't social. He just...wasn't that social with his neighbors.

Albert liked his peace and quiet.

Which he did not have right now.

The bells got louder the closer he got to the corner of the room. Ah ha! Finally. He was zeroing in on a location.

Before getting the super all the way up here, he double checked the entire area around the noise. There were a few storage boxes filled with books stacked against the wall. Things he hadn't gotten to his storage unit yet. But no furniture or appliances to move and check behind thankfully. Once he'd moved the boxes—and double checked inside to make sure the bells weren't somehow coming from there—he set his ear to the wall, listening intently.

Yes! The bells were definitely louder here. He was sure he'd found them. And they were definitely in the wall.

So weird.

Okay. Time to call the super and get this fucking noise stopped. He had work to do. It did not involve going slowly insane from the near constant ting-a-ling-a-ling.

CHAPTER TWO

Unfortunately, there was some sort of water emergency on 6, so the super couldn't get to Albert immediately. Maybe not even that day. Terry said she'd try to get there before it got too late, but they weren't going to be opening any walls in the apartment until tomorrow at the earliest.

When Albert had raised his concerns that someone's pet had gotten into the walls, Terry had assured him someone would have reported that by now. Yes, same with a child. No, Albert, especially with a child. There'd be panic. No person or pet was in the wall. Probably just some old toy a kid had dropped through a doorjamb or something and the vibrations of the subway under the building were setting it off.

It was a very reasonable explanation. And honestly, that reasonable explanation set Albert's mind at rest. A little. But since he wasn't going to get any sleep or work done as long as those bells were making noise, he really couldn't wait until tomorrow. After more nagging, whining and begging, Terry relented and said she'd come up and check as soon as she could.

Albert tried to go back to work. Failed miserably. Went and tapped on the wall a few times. If something tapped back, he was going to freak out, but maybe then he could get Terry up here quicker.

Nothing tapped back. Just more ting-a-ling-a-ling.

Something of a relief. Didn't help him get any work done.

When his noise cancelling headphones proved to be just as inadequate to blocking the sound during the day as they'd been at night, he finally took himself from the apartment and went for a walk. He wasn't getting anything done today. Might as well take in some fresh air.

He bundled up in his thick wool coat, hat, scarf, gloves, heavy boots, and headed across the street and down a block to the cemetery.

The elaborate front wrought iron gates were propped open so vehicles could drive in and out. The cemetery was surrounded on three sides by a tall brick wall and a chainlink fence made up the fourth. Thick maple trees rose up over grassy hills covered in elaborate old headstones. At least in this part of the cemetery. There were more modern parts, with less elaborate headstones. But he liked this section best. People used to create art for their dead. He liked the idea of someone creating art for him to honor his life.

He paused at one headstone made to look like a pile of wood, carved out of gray stone. The details in the stack of wood were so expertly rendered, he'd had to touch the headstone once to make sure it was just rock and not actual trees. Another headstone shot up in a small obelisk made of red marble. Yet another looked an awful lot like a doorway.

That one sort of freaked Albert out. Why make a doorway for your dead relatives? Did you really want them to *use* that door?

Shivering, he moved on, walking a quiet loop around and

through the hills, letting the late afternoon sunshine get into his eyes even as the harsh cold stung his cheeks. The fresh air did feel good. Cleared his mind a little. He'd swear he could still hear the ting-a-ling-a-ling echoing in his head, but he knew that was just because of a relentless twenty-four hours of that noise pummeling his brain.

Though, as he moved deeper into the cemetery, to an even older section with less elaborate headstones with dates that went back to the eighteen hundreds, he'd swear he was hearing that sound again in real life. Not just a painful echo imprinted on his eardrums. Frowning, he left the paved road to walk through the grassy hill, passing rows upon rows of stones set into the ground. These weren't decorated in elaborate stonework and marble. This was the pauper's section of the cemetery, where they'd buried the poor souls without enough money or resources to ensure they were buried with ceremony. The headstones were basic. Marked with a name, maybe, and some dates. Not always birth and death. Sometimes just death.

And there was that one that had the birth but *no* death written in. That one always wigged him out, same as the doorway stone. Back in the day, if they knew someone's birthday, and there was a place for them in the cemetery, surely someone at least knew the *year* that person died. Made him think maybe the person hadn't actually died and was wandering around the cemetery as a vampire or zombie or something.

Although, this was New York. If there was a vampire or zombie around here somewhere, they were probably working in Manhattan, not hanging around a Queens cemetery.

Albert continued to follow the sound, deeper into the cemetery, up and over the hill to the far side near a brick wall.

No view of the road beyond, but the occasional car passing temporarily blocked the ringing sound.

If that ringing was coming from one of those grave bells, Albert was going to run away to the nearest airport, get on a plane, and fly to another country. Especially since none of these graves were recent. The ground hadn't been disturbed here in a long time and no fresh grave dirt patches showed. The idea of grave bells had always scared him, though. The thought of being buried alive and having to ring a bell, hope the grounds keepers heard it and came to unbury you even as your oxygen was running out? Argh! Very very scary.

And not anything he'd ever once thought about during these walks in the cemetery. In fact, he couldn't remember coming across grave bells anywhere here. If he'd thought about it, he'd have assumed anything like that was removed a long time ago because...well, embalming and the time of grave bells was so long ago, they were pointless now. Anyone in those graves was well dead.

But that ting-a-ling-a-ling was still sounding, driving him on. No people were back here. Not even one of the grounds keepers. The grass was still well tended and short, so this wasn't a neglected part of the cemetery. But it wasn't frequently visited by people. In fact, as he looked around, he wasn't sure he'd ever been back here either. Really was off the beaten track. Wasn't even one of the walking stone paths through here.

As he approached the sound, he made note of the fact that there were no obvious grave bells. That was a relief.

The stone he stopped at wasn't as reassuring.

Like the others, it was just a rectangular block of gray stone set into the green grass. No brass plaque with the names and dates. This one had the name and date carved into the stone. The carvings were shallow, on their way to being scrubbed away by weather erosion, but still deep enough to read.

Albert Scruddy. 1804 to 1843.

Little spooky the dead man had the same the same first name, but different last name. Not a relative. Not that any of his relatives would be buried here. Most of his family was from the west coast. Their graves were that side of the country.

He didn't see a source for the ting-a-ling-a-ling, but the sound was definitely louder here at Albert Scruddy's grave. He hunted through the grass, close to the wall, the neighboring headstones. Hoping to find someone had tossed a kid's toy over the brick wall, or maybe brought a grave decoration with bells on that had gotten blown to this side of the cemetery.

He couldn't see anything.

Maybe he really was going crazy. If Terry came up to his apartment and didn't hear the irritating bells when he did, or worse, the bells stopped until after Terry left, Albert was definitely going to check himself into a hospital. He might be having a stroke and didn't even realize. Wouldn't that be just his bad luck to die of stroke at the back of a cemetery? They wouldn't even have to take him far to bury him.

He glanced around and shivered as a cold breeze ruffled the maple leaves and made the high branches sway.

Pausing at Albert Scruddy's grave one last time, he got down on his knees and searched very carefully through the grass. There had to be a bell around here somewhere. That sound wasn't in his head. He was sure of it. He'd located the bells in his apartment. He could find them here.

He pushed aside a patch of grass… Blinked.

Then fell back on his ass and screeched.

CHAPTER THREE

Albert crab walked backward, over the top of other graves, to get away from the…the…

He wasn't even sure what he'd seen. Whatever it was, it wasn't natural.

The thing, whatever it was, rose up out of the grass next to Albert Scruddy's grave. It wasn't big. Maybe the size of a subway rate, which was large for a rat, but in the grand scheme of things not huge. And it was very white. Not a rat though. It didn't have fur. Albert was pretty sure that was skin or scales but it was hard to tell because mostly he was scanning his peripheral vision for escape routes.

The thing wasn't moving fast, but there was a coiled-ness to it that made Albert think it probably *could* move fast if it wanted to.

There was something like a head. A rounded bit on top of a sort of oblong body. There were six legs. No tail. The headlike bit had eyes that were huge and round and black with a pinpoint of pink in the center. No ears or nose that he could see.

But there was a mouth.

The mouth was the reason Albert climbed to his feet. The mouth was the reason Albert kept backing away from the thing.

The mouth was filled with teeth. Sharp sharp teeth. Black teeth. Inside a very white, bulbous body.

He again thought of subway rats, but this was as if one had gone really, horribly wrong. Mutated beyond what a rat could possibly be.

The thing moved then. Suddenly. Just as Albert had feared. A sort of jumping lurch that landed it a whole foot closer in a blink.

Albert made a strangled sound that could well have been a scream if he wasn't having so much trouble breathing. Faced with anything else, that scream might have been embarrassing. But whatever that creature was… No shame in a scream. In fact, the scream was clawing at his throat. A real scream was going to break through at any moment.

The creature lurched forward again.

Ting-a-ling-a-ling.

Albert blinked.

The ringing bell? The bell was…the creature somehow?

The thing leapt-lurched. Ting-a-ling-a-ling.

Its mouth was open when it lurched. The sound seemed to come from its mouth more than anywhere on its body. What the hell?

Well, yes, Albert thought. This was hell. This was definitely something from hell. Except he'd never believed in hell before.

The thing lurched forward again. Another ringing sound from its open mouth.

Albert opened his mouth to scream, stumbling backward himself until he came up hard against a tree. He desperately wanted to run away. Wanted to turn and race out of the cemetery never to return. Except he didn't want to turn his back on the little creature. Did it have wings? None he could see. But those lurching leaps took it far. And the thought of it landing on him, of those black teeth sinking into him, left him so revolted and horrified he nearly threw up.

The creature leapt forward again.

Albert did scream then.

And the creature screamed.

It was the most horrible sound he'd ever heard. High pitched. Piercing. Worse than subway breaks screeching in a narrow tunnel.

He covered his ears to block out the sound, but sill that scream echoed in his brain.

The creature cut off the sound. And then…

Ting-a-ling-a-ling.

Heart pumping, adrenaline making him dizzy and pushing him to run, Albert was slow to realize. That ting-a-ling-a-ling was…

A *sound* the creature was making with its mouth. Like the scream. But, well, not as piercing. Just as horrible in its own right, but more because the consistency of it was maddening. And as he stood frozen, his back pressed up hard to the maple tree behind him, his pulse racing, the creature ting-a-ling-a-linged again.

But it stopped jumping forward.

The thing rose up on its back legs, its front four legs weaving through the air. And it gave a little wave with those feet. Then the ting-a-ling-a-ling sound came from it again. And those creepy black eyes opened wider.

What the…?

The black teeth clicked together. Which was an incredibly unnerving sound. Then the creature dropped onto all six feet and scrambled back into the grass near the gravestone, disappearing from sight.

Albert recognized that was his opening. Run! He had to run away now.

He didn't.

Panic. Curiosity. The thought that that ting-a-ling-a-ling sound had been *in* his apartment. For twenty-four hours! Whatever kept him rooted in place, he didn't take his chance to run. He just stayed pressed against the tree, his heart hammering, not daring to take his gaze off where the creature had vanished.

After a few moments, the paralysis holding him in place started to ease. It had left? Gone away? That's what he should do, too. Go away. Run. Run very fast.

Definitely moving, too. Hotel first. He'd go directly to the subway, into Manhattan. Hotel as far away from... whatever this was. And then maybe he'd move to Toronto. Or Paris. Or Tokyo. Yeah. Maybe Tokyo would be far enough away.

Instead of running, Albert pushed away from the tree and took a step closer to where the creature had disappeared. His rational brain screamed at him.

This is the part of the movie where that thing jumps out and attaches itself to your face! Where it implants an egg that later bursts out of your chest! Run, you dumb motherfucker! Run!

He did not run. He leaned down to see if he could spot the creature in the grass again. And his rational brain realized he would never be able to snort-laugh at how suicidally stupid people in movies could be again. If he survived. Which his rational brain seriously doubted.

But... Curiosity had Albert taking one more staggering step toward where the creature had vanished.

And when it leapt-lurched back into view, only a few feet from him, he screamed again.

The creature didn't mimic his scream this time. It rose up on its hindlegs again, waved its front legs. The ting-a-ling-a-ling sound escaped its mouth. And it bounced back to the ground.

Landing on something that crinkled.

Albert frowned. A chip bag?

A small chip bag. One of those single serve ones that came with the sandwiches he got for lunch.

A Cheetos bag.

Albert thought of those stray Cheetos he'd found in his apartment. Cheetos. Under his chair. Behind his couch.

He'd known in an unacknowledged sort of way that this creature, or one like it, had been in his apartment. The reason he wanted to run away to Tokyo. But this…this *knowing* it had been there. Under his *couch*. Eating Cheetos. That thought was almost enough to break him. This thing had been *right under him* while he ignorantly sat on his couch watching hockey.

The creature sat on its hind legs again. And let out another ting-a-ling-a-ling. Then dropped onto the Cheetos bag again.

The panic that had seized Albert's thinking eased its grip enough for him to recognize that this was…not aggressive behavior from the creature. Despite its horrifying appearance and very sharp black teeth, it had not, in fact, jumped onto his face and started eating him. It hadn't done anything at all that could be called an attack.

It wasn't even getting all that close to him.

Albert took a step closer to the creature. The creature scrambled back a foot. Then forward again and stomped on the Cheetos package. Making it crinkle. Then back a foot.

Well shit. It…it wanted Cheetos?

"If I get you more chips," he said, his voice tight and high and rusty sounding, "will you leave my apartment?"

Ting-a-ling-a-ling.

Not a yes or a no. How to interpret that sound?

Okay. Well.

Cheetos it was. Because buying a bag of chips was infinitely better than that thing eating his face.

Whatever the hell it was.

CHAPTER FOUR

Albert answered the door to Terry later that evening. She was an older woman, thick around the middle but overall, very fit. A few inches shorter than Albert with a mop of silver-gray hair she kept up in a bun while working.

"Let's look at this bell issue," she said.

"It's fine," Albert said quickly. "Not hearing it anymore. Whatever it was, it must have...I don't know. Fallen down a story maybe? One of the neighbors might hear it eventually."

Terry sighed and nodded. "Old buildings, right? Okay. Well, just let me know if you hear it again and we'll look at it. The situation on Six seems to be better so unless there's another emergency, I'm available." She tapped a finger to her forehead and abled off.

Albert quickly closed the door and watched through the peephole to make sure Terry left. Then he let out a sigh.

Ting-a-ling-a-ling.

"I'm not supposed to have pets," he said, looking down. "Actually, the problem is if I *do* get a pet, I have to fill out a lot of paperwork for the co-op, and they're going to want to know what kind of animal you are. Which I can't answer. So better you just keep quiet. Okay?"

Ting-a-ling-a-ling.

Not that Albert could think of the little thing as a pet. He was still adapting to its weirdly smooth skin and big eyes with the pink in the center and six legs and no ears but mostly that mouth full of black teeth.

Which were currently covered in Cheeto dust, giving its mouth an orange cast. Which, frankly, was better than the black.

It had followed him home. Or more that it had appeared back in his home after he'd returned with a big bag of Cheetos when he couldn't find it in the cemetery again. There it was, this time sitting in the middle of his living room floor. It had seen the bag of chips and sat up, its front four feet waving.

Really really reminding him of some sort of weird dog.

He narrowed his eyes down at the little beasty now. "How did you learn that begging thing? You've been watching other people's pets?"

Ting-a-ling-a-ling

"That's what I thought."

He moved back into the living room, already pulling out his phone to make an order of Cheetos that would be delivered regularly. The little creature was almost all the way through his bag, and Albert had bought him a big bag.

"We'd better figure out what else you eat, too. Can't just live on Cheetos, right?" Plus, Albert was still a tiny bit worried about what the beasty ate when it wasn't eating Cheetos. But after what he'd seen, he was less worried about the little guy eating his face.

Ting-a-ling-a-ling.

"Probably gonna need to name you something to," Albert muttered as he scheduled a recurring order.

He glanced toward the couch, which he'd pulled away from the wall a few inches. He'd missed that hole when searching for the source of the bell sound. But no one could blame him. It hadn't looked like hole at the time. Not until he saw the creature stick a paw into the wall then jerk it out quickly and make a very rapid-fire ting-a-ling noise. A noise that sounded remarkably distressed.

Albert had gotten down on his stomach to bring his head level with the spot and, feeling ridiculous, had stuck his head into the wall.

Through an invisible hole that somehow led into a different place that was not the neighbor's apartment. It wasn't New York at all.

It was…somewhere else.

He'd spent exactly twenty seconds blinking at the somewhere else when he spotted something large and noisy on the horizon. Something with tentacles and wings. Something that swooped down and picked up a smaller something from the horizon. Something that tore that smaller something into pieces that sprayed pink across the white sky.

Albert jerked his head back through the hole and into his apartment, his pulse pounding. The landscape in that other world only really sank in after he'd stopped looking at it, when he could think beyond the spray of pink and the scream of pain abruptly cut off.

Spires of white stone. Patches of black trees. The sky a faded blue that looked washed out, nearly white itself. The distant something on the horizon had looked like cross between a dragon and a hippopotamus, with black skin and tentacles and wings. Not close enough to see its teeth, for which Albert was grateful. Watching it tear something to pieces had been more than enough.

In his memory, he saw faint touches of pink and blue throughout the landscape, but he wasn't sure if he'd *really* seen those colors or not. And because his curiosity seemed to want to be the death of him that day, he stuck his head back through the hole, despite the distressed ting-a-linging from the creature.

One of those large, black tentacled beasts swooped overhead. A piercing bell sound, much deeper and louder than ting-a-ling, the sort of sound Albert felt in his chest. A rapid breeze swept across his face. And the black creature dropped out of the sky.

Albert jerked back as the beast on the other side of the hole rushed toward him, close enough for Albert to see its teeth. White teeth. Very very white teeth coated in pink blood.

The little creature in his living room pulled him back through the hole, using four of its six legs to somehow shove Albert to one side before the monster on the other side took his head. But only barely. The after-vision of that hideous creature coming for his face, its white teeth snapping, had left him sitting wide-eyed on the floor for a long time, staring at his new friend-pet who'd pushed him free.

They'd blocked the hole with a lot of cardboard and duct tape after that, then pushed the couch back against the wall.

It might take him some time before he could sit on the couch again, though. Just long enough to make sure nothing else came through.

Since that discovery—and blocking the hole—Albert and the little creature had settled into a sort of peaceful neutrality. He didn't think sending it back to its own world was a good idea—at least the little creature didn't like the idea at all. It had faded into the wall, nearly disappearing, when Albert had suggested it might be better off in its own world, even with those dangerous monsters there. Its camouflage was so good, Albert realized that was why he couldn't find it earlier, despite the ting-a-ling sounds. It had literally blended *into* his wall.

After a moment, it had reappeared and made a very distressed ting-a-linging again, so Albert had let it stay. He couldn't bring himself to kick the little guy out after it had saved his life anyway.

And it didn't seem to be dangerous, especially when compared to the tentacled creature. At least, not very. It only used those black teeth to each Cheetos. So far.

"You're not going to eat my face off if we run out of Cheetos, are you?" he asked, just to make sure.

A very definitive headshake and a ting-a-ling-a-ling.

Albert blinked, wondering where it had learned the headshake thing. Wondering how it understood him.

Well, if he'd inherited a being from a different realm, he supposed it could have been worse. Maybe if he figured out what all the ting-a-linging meant, or the creature discovered a better way to communicate with him, they'd figure it all out.

The little guy blinked up at him with its huge black eyes, that winking pupil of pink ever so slightly less disturbing than it had been earlier in the day.

"Yeah, I need a name for you. Calling you 'the creature' all the time feels rude. Especially after you saved my bacon from that monster in your realm. So, what do you think? Since I can't understand your ting-a-lings to get your real name, if you have one, what do you think would suit?"

Ting-a-ling-a-ling.

"Too long. What if we shorten it? How do you like Ting Ling?"

The creature hopped up onto its back legs, waving its

front four legs in the air, then leapt high enough to reach the ceiling and zinged around the room at a speed that made it blur. When it stopped running, it paused in front of Albert. Looking up at him with those weird eyes in a way that Albert was tempted to call…happy.

"Okay, then." Looked like he had a new pet. One who was just as creepy looking as a mouse and yet somehow a lot less disturbing. Albert would probably wonder about that at some point.

But for now, he was happy to give his new friend a home.

His friend Ting Ling.

SOPHIE SAVES THE WORLD

CHAPTER ONE

To say I was stunned that first time, when Gerald walked through my bathroom wall while I was sitting on the toilet, would be an understatement. Looking back on it now, I'm not sure why I was so surprised. It was just the sort of thing Gerald would do. But at the time, not knowing Gerald like I do now, I think I was justified in my shock.

"You have to come back with me," Gerald said as I stared from my perch. "You have to save my world."

Seeing as how I was sitting on the toilet with my mouth hanging open and my jeans around my ankles, I wasn't feeling like the "world-saving" type. The fact that Gerald was only three foot tall, green skinned, with pointed ears and a thin tail with a little flat flag at the end didn't help my self-confidence.

Logic said you couldn't have an LSD flashback if you'd never taken LSD. Staring at Gerald, I wasn't so sure.

"Well," Gerald said, tapping a large webbed foot against my in-need-of-cleaning white tiled floor.

"Well," I echoed. Though, I'm not sure my mouth closed when I spoke because what I said sounded more like, "wah."

"Well. Would you get a move on, please. We have an entire world to save."

"I think you've got the wrong person."

There in the middle of my white and green bathroom, with too many of my products on the sink counter because I'd run out of room in my medicine cabinet, with the blue towel on the towel rack needing to be tossed into the laundry, with a small pile of clothes in the corner that I'd kicked there after changing after work last night, I did not feel like the sort of person these things happened to.

I wasn't particularly brave. Or smart. I had no superpowers. Really, I was just an ordinary woman who worked tending bar and tried her best every day. But not… world saving material.

This had to be a mistake. I was absolutely sure it was a case of mistaken identity.

And it was a really weird bit of bad luck that this mistaken identity was taking place in my messy bathroom. While I was sitting on the toilet.

Suddenly, so fast I blinked, Gerald stepped close and stuck his face up to mine, staring at me with a remarkably normal pair of brown eyes. I frowned at those brown eyes, and the reality of a short, green…something being in my face while I was *indisposed*, as my grandmother would say.

Why did Gerald smell like peppermint? I still don't know. And if he knows, he's never told me.

"Nope," he said after a minute. "You're the one all right."

It took me a while, but I finally gathered my wits enough to noticed I was sitting on the toilet with a strange—man?—a strange *he* anyway in the bathroom with me. And that I should really change that dynamic.

"Would you mind turning around please?" My voice broke on "around."

He scowled. "Why? You're not gonna run, are you? We don't have time for running away."

"No. No. I'd just like to stand up now."

"Oh!" Bushy eyebrows rose into a mop of black hair, and he turned his back to me.

While I sorted myself out, trying to ignore my burning cheeks, I asked, "Uhm… What are you?"

"Gerald."

"Nice to meet you, Gerald. I'm Sophie. But…exactly what are you, Gerald?"

"You ready yet?"

"Just about. Don't turn around!" As soon as I had my jeans buttoned, I felt better. Well not *better* because there was still a short, green…something in my bathroom named Gerald. But at least I no longer had my jeans around my ankles. Progress. After a deep breath that was a little hard because my jeans were tight, I said, "Ready. Are you ignoring my question?"

"Come on." He grabbed my hand and the warmth of his skin surprised me. Not sure why I thought he'd be cold. Probably the green tint. The color reminded me of those colorful geckos that live in rainforests.

Gerald started walking toward the bathroom wall, a blank space in the green and white tiles. Not the bathroom door. The wall.

I jerked back, pulling us both to a stop. "Wait. What are you doing? I can't walk through a wall."

He took a long, impatient breath, and turned back to me. "You can if you're holding my hand. As you might have guessed by now, I'm a magical creature. At least as far as your world is concerned. In my world, I'm perfectly normal."

The condescending patience in his voice made me bristle. I wasn't a genius, but I wasn't stupid either. "You still haven't told me what you are." I tugged my hand free and crossed my arms, tapping a foot.

"We don't..." He paused, considered me. Shaking his head in disgust, he said, "I should have known. He always picks the stubborn ones."

"Who?"

"The Right Man." I opened my mouth to ask, but he held up a hand. "You'll meet him soon enough. As for me, I'm a Heezgnome."

"Never heard of them."

"That's because we're from a different world." He said each word slowly as if speaking to a very dense child.

I was starting to feel childish as my legendary stubbornness kicked in. "You might try being a little more polite if I'm supposed to save your world. When will I be back?"

"Don't know."

"But..."

"There's a space-time difference. No one here will notice."

"How much time will pass here?"

"You do realize that if my world moves faster than yours, there's been enough time for at least twelve catastrophes to take place in the amount of time you've stood there stalling. Can we talk about this when we get there?"

"Listen, this is just weird. I don't believe you. I should leave a note. Something. My mom rings every Sunday. If I'm not here, she'll worry. Who will feed my goldfish?"

I wasn't too worried about my job. I liked tending bar all right. Lots of people. Lots of stories. Good tips when I wore tight jeans. Not too many assholes because the bouncers at our place were excellent and protective. But if I lost this current job, it wouldn't be the end of my world. Bartenders are always needed somewhere in Las Vegas.

"You'll be back before anyone notices," Gerald said again, exasperated.

"What am I supposed to do?"

"Oh for Sheekna's sake."

He grabbed my hand again, displaying an amazing amount of strength for someone only three feet tall, and jerked me forward.

We tumbled through the bathroom wall before I could shout, "Hey!"

CHAPTER TWO

*O*n the other side of my bathroom wall was the most amazing landscape I'd ever seen—because it was perfectly ordinary and could have been my neighbor's backyard. The browning grass, kept alive by a lake of water sprinkled on it every day, was pretty typical of our neighborhood. The heat pouring down from a bright blue sky and a dry, warm breeze really did make me think of home. Was I just…outside?

"Where…?"

"Come on." Gerald jerked me into motion again. I was too busy trying to pinpoint whose backyard I was in to focus on where we were going. I had a few neighbors that would call the police in a heartbeat if they saw me and a strange little green man on their property. Was I in one of those yards?

I blinked when Gerald walked us through a brick fence and we immerged into a tropical jungle, thickly scented with flowers and moss. The heady smell made me dizzy. I had a brief moment to murmur, "We could stay here," before Gerald pulled me into the base of a giant tree.

We stepped out into desert with gold sand dunes as far as I could see. I didn't even get a chance to feel the heat before Gerald pulled me into the sand. There was a split second when I couldn't breathe, and I thought I was dead.

Then we immerged into the rain.

"This is a longer trip than I expected," I gasped as rain washed sand out of my hair and soaked through my jeans and cotton t-shirt. I was not happy about the wet t-shirt part, or the damage all this jumping to new environments was doing to my hair, but given everything else it was the least of my worries.

"Okay, now where to?" The rain was cold and I was getting chilled. I hate being cold. That's why I live in the desert. Although, I could go back to that tropical jungle that smelled so good I got dizzy. I could definitely go back there.

I was expecting Gerald to walk us through another wall, or drop us down through the cobblestones at my feet. Instead, he led me down an alley between two large brick buildings, turned onto a pedestrian path that wound through what looked like a medieval German village—though I wasn't an expert. The beams across the second stories on all the buildings and the wooden roofs reminded me of Germany, though.

What did they call those kinds of buildings? There was a name for them. Couldn't think of it at that moment. I needed my phone to do a search. But my cell was at home plugged into its charger. Because I had been in the toilet. Not expecting to go on an adventure.

There probably wouldn't have been cell service there anyway.

The path ended in a small courtyard dominated by a gray stone fountain. I stared at the statue in the center of the fountain for a solid minute before I realized it was me.

The statue was standing with head high, hair flowing out

behind the woman who was apparently me, wearing jeans and a t-shirt, one of the hiking boots had a big hole in it. Water sprayed out of a globe held in the statue's open palm, filling the circular stone pool beneath.

The only real difference between the statue and me at the moment were the shoes. I was wearing tennis shoes, not hiking boots. Those were still in my closet.

"Gerald?"

"Sophie."

"What's this?"

"A fountain the people here made for you. I think they build it about ten years from now."

"Huh?"

"Time's a funny thing, Sophie," Gerald said, sounding very philosophical.

"Uh huh."

We stood there for a few more minutes getting steadily wetter and colder. I was soaked through already so it didn't much matter. But I could use a coat. There were lights on in some of the surrounding buildings, flickering orange light, but no one passed through the open courtyard or looked out a window to yell at us.

Wrapping my arms around myself, my gaze sweeping the courtyard, I finally got impatient. "What are we waiting for?"

"The alignment."

"The alignment?"

"Yes. As someone—" he glared at me, "—delayed our original schedule, we missed the last one. Now we have to wait."

Okay. Weird. But apparently, that was my life now. "Want to tell me where we're going while we wait?"

"To see The Man. The 'where' won't make any sense to you. You've never been there before."

As rain dripped off the tip of my nose, I stared at the fountain statue that looked like me. And wondered.

"Here we go." Gerald took my hand again and we were off.

He dragged me through three more settings before stopping for a breath. I looked around at the newest place, thinking I'd never complain about having more than two airport layovers again.

We were standing in the middle of a pasture of purple grass dotted with multicolored things that looked like miniature animals on sticks but were probably supposed to be flowers. The one tree I could see in the distance had round orange foliage and a florescent pink trunk. The sky was a light blue and the clouds were white. It looked like the kind of world a child would color in a coloring book.

"Is this it?" I did a single turn to take in the colorful landscape.

"Not yet. One last transition and we're there. Unfortunately, we'll have to wait here for a bit." Gerald glanced around as if nervous, his tail twitching in the bright sunshine.

I frowned, turned in a circle again, trying to figure out what had him spooked. This did not look like a dangerous place.

As we waited, Gerald's tension passed to me. I found myself watching the horizon dreading the sight of some giant monster striding toward us. Gerald started tapping his foot.

"Almost time?" I murmured.

"Almost. Won't be soon enough for me."

"Mind telling me why you're worried?"

"There are some bad things in this world. We don't want them to notice us."

"Bad as in…"

He froze, his gaze locking on something in the grass behind me. I turned slowly, hoping it was the alignment but terrified of seeing a giant snake.

What I saw horrified me more.

The little brightly colored flowers were moving. Not waving gently in the breeze. They were actually moving, in slow measured jumps on their reed thin stems. The flower heads shaped like animals were also moving, growing with every jump. Their misshapen heads twisted toward us, mouths gaping open to reveal a lot of very sharp looking teeth.

Teeth inside a flower mouth that looked vaguely like animal heads. That was bad.

"It's gonna hurt if they bite us, isn't it?" I didn't really want to know. I turned in a circle. No escape route. We were surrounded. And the no-longer-so-little flower-monsters were closing in. "Don't suppose you've got that alignment coming up anytime soon, Gerald."

"Won't be quick enough. They're picking up speed. Here." He grabbed my arm and tugged me closer to the ground.

I knelt down. "Will this help?"

"Yes." He scrambled onto my shoulders before I knew what he was doing.

"Hey! You're heavy."

"Stand up, stand up, stand up!" The panic in his voice made me stumbled upward, choking when he clamped his arms around my neck to keep his balance.

Once at my full height again, I recognized this wasn't helping me at all. "Why am I protecting you?"

"Because they probably won't like you, but they love eating Heezgnomes. Don't worry. Just don't make any sudden moves."

"Right. No sudden moves." I adjusted his legs over my shoulders so I was holding him more firmly. He'd stopped choking me, but only because his arms were wrapped around the top of my head now instead of my neck. "You do realize if they bite me, I'm going to jump and scream, and you're gonna come tumbling off."

"Don't do that!" His arms dropped back around my neck, squeezing tight.

I gagged. "If you choke me," I wheezed, "I'll pass out and you'll end up on the ground sooner." His arms loosened but only a little. "How long until the alignment?"

"Few more minutes."

"Gerald."

"Yes?"

"I don't think I'm gonna like saving your world if I have to face miniature biting animals that look like flowers."

The nearest flower animals were sniffing around my feet.

"Don't worry," Gerald said, his voice an octave higher in my ear, "we don't have anything like these flowers in my world."

"Oh good."

A little yellow flower that looked like a cross between a dog and an elephant nudged my foot. Then sharp little teeth sunk deep into my tennis shoes, and I squealed in shock. I kicked out and sent the dog-elephant flying.

Chaos erupted.

Miniature animal flowers in primary colors swarmed my feet. I screeched and jumped around, kicking and stomping, not at all worried about the flower animals I was crushing under my shoe. If they weren't been trying to eat me, I wouldn't have had to step on them.

After a minute, I realized the attack had slowed. The flower animals were backing away from me. I looked at the grass around my feet. It looked like a crayon box had melted. Even my white tennis shoes were covered in color.

"Yuck."

"You saved me. I can't believe it. He said you would..." Gerald babbled in my ear, switching between English and some language I couldn't understand.

I let him babble while I caught my breath, keeping a careful watch on the animal flowers. After all the stomping and with the carnage at my feet, they wisely stayed at a respectful distance.

Once I could breathe without wheezing, I tried to reach Gerald through all the babble. "Gerald."

More babbling. Some patting of my head. Arms still too tight around my neck, but at least he wasn't choking me anymore. Still. I needed his attention.

"Gerald!"

"What? What?"

"The alignment?"

"Oh. Right. Let me down."

"You sure?" I eyed the milling animal flowers. They'd left us a circle of space, a sort of no-man's land littered with crayon-colored flower corpses. But I didn't trust them to stay away indefinitely.

"Yeah." Gerald patted my head again. "Hurry. I don't want to miss this one."

Me neither. I knelt and let him slid off my back. Rolling my shoulders as I stood—geez, Heezgnomes were heavy for only being three feet tall!—I watched the surrounding flowers and grabbed Gerald's hand. "Are all Heezgnomes so...sturdy."

"Sturdy?"

"Weighty..." I didn't want to hurt his feelings, but also

my back hurt now and he had interrupted me in the bathroom, so my ability to be delicate with feelings was low.

"Weighty?"

"Are you supposed to be so heavy?" I huffed.

"Yes."

And we fell through the purple grass.

CHAPTER THREE

We stepped through a rock wall into a darkness. When my eyes adjusted, I saw a glowing blue pool at the center of a stalagmite and stalactite decorated cave. There were no outside lights, but torches stuck into the wall around the cavern made it easy enough to see once I got use to the dimness.

Water dripped from the ceiling along sharpened stakes of rock and a damp sheen coated the walls. The stone was imbedded with silver flecks and crystals like the inside of a geode. They sparkled and danced in the firelight from the torches.

The place had a damp scent to it, but not musty or moldy. Almost fresh for the inside of a cave, which was surprising. And the temperature was remarkably comfortable.

My clothes had dried during the last two transitions, which was good, but my jeans were still chaffing my thighs, which wasn't great for my mood. At least my t-shirt was no longer see-through.

"Are we there yet?" I asked after Gerald released my

hand. I spun in a slow circle taking in the winking silver and crystals, the enormous number of spiked rocks dropping from the ceiling.

"This is the place," Gerald said proudly.

"Cool." I frowned down at him. "Where are we?"

"My world."

"Is your world made up entirely of caverns, or is this a special place?"

"This is the place we'll meet The Right Man. And no, my world is not entirely made up of caverns."

"You could have warned me there was more than one…" I waved my hand, trying to remember the word he'd used.

"Portal?"

"That's not what you called it earlier."

"Transition. That's the movement between aligned portals. But the exits and entrances are called portals."

Interesting. Weird day. But interesting fact about the portals. "Is there more than one portal per world? Or do you just have to transition and then hike around to where you need to go?"

"Depends on the world."

That didn't entirely help, but I was too tired to ask more questions. A little mystery could be good for a girl.

I glanced down at my feet and curled my lip at all the splatters of color. "Yuck." Then I noticed my jeans. "Ah hell." I bent down, fingering one of a hundred holes in the lower leg. "These were my favorite jeans, too," I sighed.

"You look very good in them."

The new voice startled me upright. I glanced over my shoulder. "I know."

The man standing behind me chuckled. He looked human enough. Tall, dark hair, light eyes, fit. He was wearing a strange outfit—tight fitting trousers and t-shirt, which looked normal enough, covered by a long, dark cape that didn't look very normal. Probably not from my world even if he was handsome and human-looking. Or if he was from my world, he'd been away long enough to develop a new sense of style. Which involved capes.

Good for him. But also...

"Who're you?"

"This," Gerald said, moving to stand next to the man, "is The Man."

"Nice to meet you." I had no idea what else to say. Was he like...the only man here? Given Gerald was not a human man, that was actually possible. Still, a name, or title, or whatever that was just The Man was...

Well, probably not any weirder than biting animal flowers in crayon colors.

The Man grinned and put out his hand. "My real name is Devon Fitzgerald. Gerald is just fond of my title. The Right Man. Since I'm the only human here beside you, the title The Man suits."

"Okay." That answered the question about his title. He really was the only human here. Besides me, of course. Unfortunately, it was an answer that begged about a zillion more questions. Not least of which was, if he was the only human here, did that mean he was single?

"Shall we show her?" Gerald asked, before I could marshal my wits enough to ask any of my zillion questions.

"Show me what? What?" Okay, those were questions. Not any of the original zillion. But they were questions.

"The reason you're here," Devon said.

He turned and Gerald and I followed him down a damp stone corridor. We moved downhill so it felt like we were going deeper into the caves, but for all I knew we were on our way out. The scent of the place seemed a little more heavy, the damp, almost moldy smell closing in around us here. But it was really more of a mineral scent than mold. Like a hot spring. Except it wasn't too hot.

The glittering silver and crystals embedded in the dark stone continued through the tunnel, and stalactites hung from the high roof in white and brown stacks. The occasional water drip might have been irritating, but I was too keyed up. Anxious and curious all at the same time.

"Do I get a hint?"

"It'll all be clear soon enough." Devon smiled over his shoulder at me.

Okay, he did have a great smile. But my bar-honed suspicions were finally starting to kick in. I'd been too distracted by all the world-hopping to keep up an appropriate level of suspicion with Gerald. And really, after you hold a Heezgnome on your shoulders to prevent him being eaten by animal flowers, there was only so much room for worrying about motives.

But I was finally starting to worry about Devon's.

We stepped into a cavern with jewel-encrusted walls that made my mouth water. Real jewels. Not just crystals and flecks of silver. This was diamonds and emeralds and rubies and sapphires. All in one place. All embedded in the cavern's dark walls.

I'd never seen so many precious stones in one place. Not even in a jewelry store.

"Wow." I ran a finger over a sparkling emerald the size of my thumb that was so clear it looked like it had been polished and then reinserted into the wall.

"Don't suppose I could take a few of these home with me?" I murmured.

Gerald glanced at the walls, frowning. "Why? They're just rocks."

"True." I nodded. "Very pretty rocks." Devon had to know they were more than that, at least I thought he would, but if Gerald didn't know… "Very very pretty rocks."

Gerald smiled, a sort of goofy expression for a Heezgnome, and said, "Seeing as you saved my life, it's the least we can do."

Now I was suspicious of Gerald. "What's wrong with them?"

"Nothing. But if you can get one out, I'd be impressed."

I sighed. Figured. "So what do I get for saving your life and your world and being dragged out of the bathroom on this wild ride?"

"Satisfaction, of course. You'll be the savior of an entire world. There'll be statues made in your honor. You even saw one."

"Will that get me out of my job at the Buckin' Bronco?"

"Uh…"

"That's what I thought." Tending bar at the Buckin' Bronco wasn't the most glamorous job, but it paid the rent. And I'd worked worse places. All things considered, though, I'd rather have some of those diamonds.

"Here we are." Devon spun back to us in a swirl of cape and pointed to what looked like a door drawn onto the jewel encrusted walls with chalk.

A few quiet moments passed with both Devon and Gerald staring at me in a way I could only describe as…anticipatory. What they were anticipating, I couldn't guess.

Another few moments passed in silence before I realized they were waiting on something. Waiting for my reaction maybe?

"Nice drawing," I tried, scratching the back of my neck.

They exchanged a look, hesitant and worried.

"You don't know what to do?" Gerald asked. "You knew what to do with the flower animals."

"Well, that was pretty obvious. I was bigger than they were. And the natural reaction to something biting your legs is to jump away from all the biting."

"But..." Devon spread his hands. "This should be just as obvious for you."

This *what*?

I looked at the chalk-drawing doorway again. And realized it had writing across it, right through the middle. Frowning, I stepped closer to get a better look. Hey, the words were English! That was weird considering this was a completely different world that required going through portal-y things just to get here, and I was certain Gerald's first language wasn't English. The jewels embedded in the rock wall were integrated into the writing, making up the o's and sometimes part of the d's and a's.

It was pretty. The writing very gothic and elegant. Like something out of a fantasy novel.

Then I started to read.

It took me a moment to catch on. When I did, I stumbled backward. "That's a riddle!"

"Yes," Gerald said as if I should have known that already.

"I don't do riddles. You want me to solve that, don't you? Well, I really really suck at riddles. I mean it. I can't do things like that. Never could do puzzles, crosswords, anything. I was even bad at fill-in-the-blanks questions on tests."

Devon frowned. Gerald looked shocked.

"But," Gerald mutter, "but you're the one. You're supposed to save my world."

"I told you you had the wrong person." I threw my hands up in disgust. I knew this had to be a mistake. I was a bartender from Nevada. What did I know about saving worlds?

"No, this isn't right." Devon paced away from the painted door, paced back, muttering under his breath, so quietly, I wasn't sure I was supposed to be hearing him. "You're definitely the one. I'm sure of it this time. It's your face on the fountains and portraits. It's you—" He stopped abruptly when he saw my face.

I turned on Gerald. "What's going on?"

"Okay, okay." He raised two green hands and took a deep breath. "Why don't you try to solve the riddle? Eh? I mean, what can it hurt after we came all this way?"

"You went the long way didn't you," Devon said. "I wondered what was keeping you."

"She delayed us."

"Hey! You got the wrong person."

"No, I didn't. It's you. You saw the fountain—"

"You took her by one of the fountains?" The shock in Devon's voice surprised me since he'd just mentioned fountains and portraits.

"We missed our first transition, so I had to improvise, and I didn't want anyone following us." Gerald jutted out his chin and crossed his arms over his chest, looking very defiant.

"Who would be following us?" I demanded, my voice rising to echo off the jeweled cavern walls.

"No one you have to worry about now. I made sure they couldn't follow us."

"Gerald…"

"Just try to read the riddle, will you?" He spread his hands now, imploring, his big brown eyes wide and earnest.

I wasn't buying it. "Not until I get some answers."

Gerald jerked his hands into the air and let out a snarling sort of huff.

"Stubborn," Devon said.

"Typical," Gerald said.

"One of you'd better start talking or this typically stubborn world-saver is leaving." I crossed my arms over my chest this time and glared. We all knew I was bluffing about leaving. But I could definitely out-stubborn them.

I could out-stubborn a mule.

CHAPTER FOUR

Water dripping from the stalactites onto the cavern floor was the only sound that broke the tense silence. I held my tongue and stared both Devon and Gerald down, arms folded, waiting them out. They'd brought me here. They expected me to save Gerald's world. They wanted my help, they needed to start explaining. Now.

Gerald broke first. I knew they couldn't out-stubborn me.

"You want to tell her?"

"No," Devon said.

I raised a brow, the stand-off threat obvious.

"But I will," Devon relented.

"Good." I relaxed my stance. "Tell me what exactly?"

"See…" Devon started. Then hesitated. Frowned and made fist he bounced almost like he was going to start a game of rock-paper-scissors. Started again. "You see, we know you're the one who's going to save this world. They make statues and paintings of your triumphs in the future, and Heezgnomes are good about getting around in different dimensions, so we know you're the one. From the future pictures and statues. The problem is, there's these wizards."

"Wizards?" I raised my brows. "More than one?"

"Yeah. And they're powerful, and they want to control the Heezgnomes."

"Because Heezgnomes can travel between dimensions and time and stuff."

"Exactly!"

Devon looked at me like I was a genius. A genius toddler who'd just said the entire alphabet in one go. But still, a genius. Nice compliment, though, since I was far from a genius. I'd even been slow getting the full alphabet as a kid.

"So these wizards," Deven went on, "have created a bunch of...shall we say obstacles in this world. To intimidate the Heezgnomes and force them into cooperation."

"Slavery more like it," Gerald grumbled.

"And the other worlds and dimensions don't want the Heezgnomes under the control of the wizards."

"Because of the whole dimensions and time and space stuff." Sure. That made a lot of sense. I wasn't particularly keen on these wizards enslaving Gerald's people either. Pretty crappy move, you ask me. "So why don't all the other worlds get together and do something about the wizards themselves?"

Devon and Gerald both avoided my gaze, looked at the ground between their feet, the walls... I was expecting one of them to start whistling at any moment.

"What?" I growled. "What!" My voice echoed off the high ceiling again.

"Well," Gerald said, "most of the known worlds have... sort of...crumpled under the wizards' intimidation. We're one of the last worlds holding out."

"Magic," Devon said, "the kind of magic the wizards have, is pretty rare in the multi-verses. There are other magical creatures, but the wizards are one of the few to really take hold of magic and make it work against the natural grain. So to speak."

"For the rest of us," Gerald said, "what you might call our magic is just part of who we are. We don't gather and manipulate our skills, they just sort of happen. Like breathing. I move between dimensions the way fish on your planet move through water. They don't control or increase their ability to swim with study. They just swim."

"The wizards, on the other hand," Devon said, "have learned how to gather magic, to manipulate and use it. And once they figured it out, they used it to subjugate the other worlds."

"How'd they get to the other worlds to subjugate them without a Heezgnome?" I was starting to get the general picture, and it was pretty bad to be fair, but I still didn't get what it had to do with me. "Also, why haven't they come to Earth, to my world?" Wizards would walk right over the humans of Earth, I was sure.

Another look passed between Devon and Gerald. "They haven't come to Earth because they can't get there," Devon said.

"And they can't get there because the Heezgnome that's working with them doesn't know where it is," Gerald finished.

"They have a Heezgnome working for them?" I paused to let that sink in. "So they could just show up at any minute?" My voice squeaked on the last word.

Wizards with magic? And a Heezgnome working with them? And all of them looking to subjugate all the other Heezgnomes! We hadn't even gotten to what the wizards' obstacles were yet.

I was in over my head and about to drown. I wasn't even the swimming fish. Magic was as foreign as all the portaling stuff was to me. I didn't *have* magic to fight back with. What the hell were they expecting me to do? Why did they think *I* could help with something so immense?

I started to breath harder and had to bend forward, resting my hands on my knees as I tried not to pass out. They definitely had the wrong girl. I was hyperventilating at the thought of all this. I was *not* anyone's savior.

"They can't get here," Gerald said, his tone soothing. He patted the air just above my shoulder as if he was trying to comfort me.

"These are the Heezgnome's sacred caves," Devon said. "The caves are protected in a way none of us understand. Only a few can come here directly through the portal— Gerald, me, a few Heezgnome high elders. The Heezgnome working for the wizards can't pass through the portal, so neither can the wizards."

"They'd have to come in the long way," Gerald said, still in that soothing attempt at a reassuring tone.

"Long way?" I glanced up to meet Gerald's gaze.

He shrugged. "From the outside. It's a really long way down here, though. Takes a few days."

That didn't make me feel better. Straightening, I looked up at the ceiling and thought about cave-ins. But if I thought about that too long, I was going to hyperventilate again.

"So where do you come in to all this, Devon?" I asked, needing a distraction from the potential of being trapped under all that rock. "You're no Heezgnome."

"He's The Right Man," Gerald said, no longer using his soothing tone. "I told you that already."

"But what does he *do*?"

"I'm sort of a prophet to the Heezgnomes," Devon said, a little shyly. "I'm from Earth, too. I taught the Heezgnomes English and have helped lead them to you."

I scowled at Devon for a long moment. "How did you end up here?"

"Accident." He shrugged. "Slipped through a portal with a Heezgnome just passing through. I was so shocked when I saw him that I reached out to touch him and before we knew it, we were tumbling into this world. Took a bit of time, but when we could communicate and I realized what the problem was here, I promised to help them find you. I work as an advisor to the king on a day-to-day basis. That's where the term The Right comes from—I serve on the king's right hand. The Man is because I am one. Obviously." More shy shrugging.

"Obviously." I was too overwhelmed to be charmed by all the shy shrugging. But Devon didn't seem to notice my deadpan tone.

"My primary duty, though, has been to find you," he finished.

"Why me?" I'd never asked that question before. I didn't believe in it. I thought it was a stupid question to ask. I mean, why not you? But this wasn't really a "why is this happening to me" question. This was a "why do you think this has anything to do with me" question.

I was literally no one. Just a bartender in Vegas doing her best to get by. This was so much more and I had no idea why anyone would think *I* could save a world.

"Because," Devon said, "you're the face on the sculptures. You're the person in the future portraits. The Heezgnomes can move around in time a bit. But because time is nebulous and weird, depending on now, it's a little hard to say if where they've been is the real future or a potential time or no time at all."

"Huh?"

"Let's just say, we knew who you were supposed to be. We just had to find you."

"How did you find me?"

Devon's face flamed bright red. I narrowed my eyes. Gerald cleared his throat.

"Uhm, well, we sort of knew you were supposed to be a bartender so I've been, uhm, I've been…"

"You've been barhopping?"

"Yes."

Why he was so embarrassed I couldn't imagine. He wouldn't be the first man to go barhopping looking for a woman. I wondered what he'd been doing during all that barhopping to be so embarrassed.

Then I remembered his story about following a Heezgnome into a portal. And a strange idea occurred to me. "How long have you been here?"

"I slipped through the dimensions when I was eight."

"You've been here, without humans, since you were eight?" He had to be in his late twenties. At least. What had happened to his parents? Didn't he have anyone back home that would miss him? Eight years old was…was a baby. "Weren't you lonely for home?"

"Sometimes. Not much. And when I was, they took me home and I remembered why I was happy to leave."

That hinted at not nice things about his family. I was curious enough to want to ask, reluctant to know the truth enough I didn't.

"Besides," he went on, "with the way the dimensions work, I was aging here but when I returned to Earth, everyone who'd been my age was younger than me. The first time I went back, the one friend I'd had was nine and I was nearly twelve." He shrugged as if it didn't matter.

I still thought it sounded lonely. And also maybe a little scary. "Will that happen to me?"

"No," Gerald assured me. His gentle tone surprisingly reassuring. "I'll make sure you go back often enough."

The relief made me smiled. Despite everything, I found myself having kind thoughts toward Gerald. I wouldn't say our introduction, with him catching me out on the toilet, was what one might call the "start of a beautiful friendship" type material. But, I don't know, I was starting to think of Gerald as a…well, not friend yet. But someone I could actually like when he wasn't driving me bananas.

And I sure didn't want his people to become slaves to wizards that might show up on Earth next.

"Okay. I understand you believe I'm the person who's supposed to save your world. I still think you have the wrong person. Despite what the fountains look like. But since I've come all this way…"

Gerald was grinning and pulling me closer to the chalk door before I could finish my sentence. "Just read it," he said. "I'm sure you'll be able to solve it."

"Is this by one of the wizards?" I scowled at the jewel embellished writing, the elaborate script.

"No. A Heezgnome seer did this, nearly a century ago. He'd been our king's councilor before Devon became The Right."

"But this is in English." I'd assumed the English was because of Devon and the writing was more recent since he'd said he was the one who'd taught the Heezgnomes English.

"We know. That's one of the mysteries the seer wouldn't explain to me," Devon said. He also moved closer to read the riddle.

He smelled surprisingly nice. Like expensive, subtle cologne. How did a human in a different dimension get cologne? For a few beats, all I could do was breath in that scent. Then I shook my head and went back to the riddle. Mind on the job at hand. That was me.

Supposedly someone who could save a whole world.

I didn't snort out loud at the idea. But I sort of wanted to save the world.

For the second time, I read through the riddle, and this time I tried not to panic.

In the days before the darkest dawn, right after the skylights die, the seeker's name will ring the hall, and shouts will bring her fame. If days were night and nights were dead, what would be left? Only she said.

"I don't get it." I sighed, the panic creeping in again. I shook my head hard and reread the riddle. "That first part, that's probably about me—or whoever's supposed to save this world. Maybe we're supposed to shout my name?"

"But then what's the rest mean?" Devon leaned closer, squinting at the writing. "And what's all that about the skylights dying?"

I shrugged. "No idea. Told you I was bad at riddles." I stared a bit longer, reread the rhyme. Again. Wondered.

Time passed as I stared at the elegant script, the winking jewels. I don't know how much. Not, like, a year or anything. But longer than a minute. In my head, I was trying to ignore the voice that kept telling me I couldn't do this. That they had the wrong person. I let my gaze skim over the words, mulling.

Then something occurred to me. Except... "It couldn't be that easy."

No. It couldn't be. There was no way that was the answer. Anyone could get that answer. Probably a lot faster than it had taken me. Which was why it was probably wrong.

"What?" Gerald asked.

"You understand it?" Devon said at the same time.

"No. That just can't be right. It's too easy. You guys would have gotten it already. It has to be trickier than that. It's a whole riddle. Riddles are supposed to be tricky. Aren't they?"

"Well, you are meant to open this door," Devon said, voice coxing and soft as if he was afraid to bring me out of some trance or something. "Maybe it is that easy."

"Just give it a try," Gerald urged.

Okay. Guess it couldn't hurt. I took a deep breath and shouted, "Only!"

For a long minute nothing happened. My shoulders drooped. Yup. They had the wrong girl. "I knew it couldn't be—"

Then the ground started to rumble. I stumbled against Devon. Who was kind enough to cushion my fall when we both hit the ground. Hard. Devon let out a grunt that was maybe not complimentary.

"Sophie," Gerald shouted, reaching for me.

And the lights in the cavern went out.

The sound of my name echoed like a million voices trying to talk over each other.

I might have screamed in the sudden darkness. I couldn't swear to it. There was too much rumbling noise from rocks shivering and cracking. Bad sounds. Very very bad sounds. I was aware of Devon holding me tighter, which would have been nice if I wasn't terrified of a cave-in.

A loud cracking noise almost like thunder sounded close by. I felt Gerald stumble against us and I pulled him close, clinging to him so I wouldn't lose him in the dark. All three of us huddled on the ground, clinging to each other.

Another crack that made my entire body contract as fear closed my throat. Light flashed in the confined space, dazzling me. I squeezed my eyes shut against the glare but spots still danced behind my eyelids.

Then the shaking stopped. And the cracking noises quieted.

Darkness settled around us.

CHAPTER FIVE

A long, echoing, quiet moment passed with only the smells of rock dust, peppermint, and Devon's subtle cologne surrounding me in the dark. It took the full length of that moment to realize the reason it was dark was because I had my eyes squeezed shut.

Since it didn't *feel* like I was being crushed under a mountain—just Gerald and really he wasn't *that* heavy—I blinked open my eyes.

Before I could fully understand what I was seeing, Gerald was up and jumping around.

"I knew it! I knew it! You're the one. You're going to save my world."

Slowly, I climbed to my feet and edged toward the room behind the rock rubble that had once been the painted door. Dust filtered through the air, in the flickering torch light from the outer chamber. Inside, the light was bright enough I couldn't see past the rectangular opening. I had to climb over the pile of rocks blocking the entrance, my rainbow splattered shoes starting a rain of smaller pebbles, but was too stunned to think about it.

I'd solved the riddle. I'd done it! Sort of. I had a feeling Gerald helped with his startled yelp of my name. But still. We'd done it. The door was open. How had we...how had *I* managed that with my complete lack of riddle skills?

Once inside the brightly lit room, my breathing stopped. When my chest started to hurt, I gasped. Breathing again didn't really help my shock.

In front of me was a gray stone pillar, about waist high on me. The stone was simple but jewel encrusted so it looked like the walls of the cavern. Other than the jewels there was no writing or designs on the side of the pillar that I could see. But on top of it...

On top of the pillar...a sword.

All the light in the room was coming from the sword. Around the glare, I could see it was a beautiful piece of weaponry. The hilt had a red leather grip crisscrossed by silver wire. The guard was a half-moon of intricately woven silver designs. The sword itself glowed green-silver, and what looked to be writing ran along its length.

"Holy cow," I murmured.

Beside me, Gerald whistled. "Would you look at that? Wonder what you're supposed to do with that."

I blinked and turned to face him. He was staring at the sword, so he missed my wide-open mouth and obvious expression of extreme surprise. "Wait. What? You mean I'm supposed to *use* that thing? Cause, uh, yeah, I've never handled a sword in my life."

I spun to fully face Gerald, ready to launch into another round of "you have definitely got the wrong girl," when a tapestry on the far wall stopped me and I snapped my mouth shut.

The tapestry was made up of bright, colorful threads in bold colors and showed a scene of a knight standing on the neck of a four-foot-long dragon. The dragon was a thick bodied dragon with two wings, a long tail, raised nostrils, and a sort of bluish green scale color. I looked closer at the knight's foot, firmly resting on the middle of the dragon's long neck.

He seemed to be wearing…tennis shoes.

Tennis shoes splattered in a weird array of rainbow colors.

I let my gaze travel up the knight's silver armor, move higher, along the length of the green silver sword—the real version of which was still lighting the room—all the way up to a very familiar face.

I rubbed my eyes. Didn't change the image.

"That's me." I wanted to shout but somehow it came out a whisper. "You guys don't expect me to kill a dragon. Right?" My eyes widened as I glanced down at Gerald. "Right?!"

"No, no! See the dragon is still alive." Gerald pointed to the open eyes and gnashing teeth.

Long teeth. Pointy teeth.

"Are you sure?" My voice squeaked. That was embarrassing but also very appropriate given the situation.

"Yeah," Gerald said, nodding his head frantically. "Sure. You just need to vanquish the dragon. The wizards didn't specify killing it."

Obstacles.

And one of the obstacles was a dragon.

I stared at the tapestry for a long time. How did one go about vanquishing a four-foot dragon without killing it? Stomping on little flower animals trying to eat me was one thing, but I wasn't sure I was up to the task of vanquishing a dragon—either emotionally or physically.

But I had solved a riddle, hadn't I? Sort of. If I could solve a riddle, maybe I *could* vanquish a dragon?

After a few minutes of silent staring, I noticed something strange about the armor I was wearing in the tapestry. It looked...generic. Awkward. Like it could have belonged to anyone. It certainly didn't fit *me* well.

An idea slowly seeped in past my numb confusion. And I remembered something Gerald had said when we first met.

"You told me The Man always picks stubborn ones." I glanced down at Gerald who was very obviously not looking at me. "In the bathroom when I wouldn't leave with you. What did that mean? How many 'ones' have there been?"

Gerald scuffed his feet. I turned on Devon. He focused his attention on his fingernails.

"And you said earlier that you were sure you were right about me being the one this time. *This time*." I crossed by arms over my chest as they both continued to look at everything in the room but me. "One of you'd better start talking or the dragon isn't gonna be the first one to feel that blade."

Gerald swallowed audibly.

Devon sighed. "Okay. See. All right. Thing is... See... Those future fountains and pictures? They're pretty...nebulous."

"Nebulous?"

"Like time," Devon said.

"The future isn't set," Gerald cut in. "That's the problem. Those future pictures and fountains and stuff? They...change depending on our now."

I pursed my lips and nodded, staring hard at Gerald while he desperately avoided my gaze. "So you're saying you could have brought absolutely anyone here, and the fountain we passed would have had their face?" I wasn't shouting. Yet. But I had that tone. That quiet tone that warned future shouting was eminent.

"No," Devon said, edging a few steps away from me. "Not quite. When we get it completely wrong, the statues show birds or something." He looked around the room like he was hunting for an escape route. Smart man. "That's when we know to just return to woman to her home."

"So," I said, slowly. "You've been prowling bars." I poked at Devon who took another step backward. "Looking for potential world-savers. And you—" I spun to face Gerald who'd also been creeping back away from me. He froze when I glared at him. "You have been kidnapping these women and bringing them here. And any one of them could have been your savior?"

"No." Gerald spoke with such absolute certainty.

"No what?" I asked, my voice low.

"No, none of the others could have been the savior."

"Why not?"

"None of them solved the riddle."

"What?"

"None of the others solved the riddle. Not right anyway. Some got into this room. But the sword wasn't here for any of them. And the tapestry showed a completely different scene to the dragon scene."

"The sword wasn't here? How could it not be here?"

"We don't know." Devon edged closer again, though he still looked ready to bolt if my temper rose. "This is the first time, in all the years I've been searching, that I've seen the sword. I was told only the savior of this world would be able to open the door *and* see the sword."

"So you see," Gerald said. "You *are* the one who will save my world." He puffed up his chest, giving me a smug look. "I never doubted it. Not from the beginning."

"Yes you did." But there wasn't any heat in my voice. I blinked at the tapestry again. "So... I really am supposed to save your world from all these wizardly obstacles?" It still didn't sound right. Still didn't sound like something *I* was destined for.

But, apparently, the magic sword and doorway thought differently.

"'Fraid so," Devon said. He reached out and touched my hand, a brief but comforting gesture.

I surprised myself by not pulling away. He did really smell good. "Okay then." I nodded and glanced around the chamber, lit a pale green by the glowing sword. Jewels embedded in the dark rock winked in the sword light, casting little rainbows around the room. "So... What do I do now? If I'm really supposed to do this, where do I start?"

"The dragon," Devon said. He moved to one side, leaving a clear path between the sword and me. "You have to choose this, Sophie. You have to take up the sword."

I hesitated. I didn't want to be the savior of Gerald's world. I didn't want to be here at all.

Did I?

Would I rather go back behind the bar, instead? Going nowhere, doing nothing?

Waiting for something to happen?

I spread my days between work, a few friends, my mom, and magazines. I didn't actually know where I wanted to go, what I wanted to do besides tend bar. Even that was starting to get old.

The sword's green-white light brightened and sent another wash of rainbows jumping around the room.

I stared at the sword. "How many obstacles are there?"

"About twenty," Gerald said.

"Will I be home in time to call my mom?"

"I promised you would be. You will. I'll take you back

and bring you here again as often as you need to. Shorter route this time. So long as you don't delay us again."

I looked down into Gerald's perfectly ordinary brown eyes in his very unordinary green face and thought, I don't want his world to be run by wizards. I don't want them to enslave the Heezgnomes.

And I could stop it.

Did I believe their story? They'd lied to me... Well, no, technically, they'd just left selective things out earlier. But they hadn't been completely honest with me. Maybe the wizards weren't so bad? Maybe that four-foot dragon was just misunderstood?

Maybe I'd gone mad a few hours earlier.

An echo of footsteps sounded down the corridor and a faint scent of sulfur wafted through the doorway. "Don't tell me," I said. "That's the dragon."

Devon and Gerald's eyes widened at the sound. A dead giveaway.

"So what's it going to be, Sophie?" Gerald asked, his gaze locking with mine. "Will you help us?"

"Do I trust you, Gerald?"

"No. But will you help us?"

His honest answer made me smile. "I still think you've got the wrong person."

He smiled back. "That's because you're stubborn."

The steps sounded closer. The scent of sulfur got stronger. The floor shivered and dust filtered down from the stalactite-free ceiling.

I crossed back to the sword and took hold of the hilt. To my surprise, I lifted it with ease. After a few practice swings, which I considered pretty decent considering I'd never held a sword before, I turned to my about-to-be-recruited-assistant-world-saviors and said, "Shall we go see how to vanquish a dragon?"

As it turned out, vanquishing a dragon wasn't as hard as it sounded. The dragon's name is Margaret. We posed for the tapestry on my next visit.

HOURGLASS THROUGH THE CATS EYES

A DESTINY CATS STORY

CHAPTER ONE

*E*rica Randal pushed into her small Chicago apartment, arms full of books, her mind deep in thought on her current research project. She also had some lectures to prepare for next month, to get ahead of herself, and a meeting with her faculty supervisor tomorrow to prepare for. The semester had been a little more difficult than she'd anticipated. Not because the work was beyond her skill set or because she didn't love her social history focus.

No, the difficulty had more to do with the man standing in the middle of her living room by the large, and growing, cat tree.

She sighed deeply at the sight of him. Not that he wasn't nice to look at. He was. Maybe a little too handsome really. Tall, black hair, blue eyes, pale skin. He was dressed in his other-realm clothes, though. The well-worn brown leather pants and loose white shirt, the leather belt strapped low on his hips.

The sword hooked to that belt.

"What now?" She dropped her pile of research books on

the coffee table in the middle of her living room, gently, because…well books.

The apartment wasn't a very large place. Just the living room with one huge window overlooking the tree lined road, a single bedroom just large enough for her queen-sized bed and a standing dresser, a galley style kitchen to one side of the living room, and a bathroom that was only big enough for a shower stall. No tub.

The place had felt perfectly comfortable when she was the only one living here. And the rent was good, affordable on her university salary.

Eventually, though, she was going to have to get something bigger. She already had the three cats. That was at the upper limit of what the building allowed, and she'd been a little less than honest with her landlord when she'd mentioned getting cats. But since Galahad could look like this now in this realm, she could pretend she only had two cats if the landlord dropped by.

"Jilly needs you at the temple," Galahad said.

His voice was a deep rumble, one that almost carried a purr. In his cat form, he had soft black fur with a few white patches on his chest and face, but those deep blue eyes stayed the same. After a few months of this, of starting her training with her Aunt Jilly, and Galahad moving in with her, and the cat tree, and the…destiny stuff, she still found it disconcerting how similar Galahad's eyes were in both forms. She wasn't even sure why.

Two other cats wove out from the depths of the cat tree. The tree itself looked ordinary if quite large. Unlike Jilly's light tan tree, Erica's had started out a dark blue color, the platforms and rug material covering the posts slightly different shades of blue that gave the tree a sort of depth. It was covered in cat hair of course, but she'd ended up with three cats with darker hair so it was probably good the tree wasn't a lighter color.

One of the two cats, the short-haired calico with a lot more brown and black than white, leapt up onto one of the taller posts, settling in a seated position on the round platform, her long tail wrapped around her legs, her green-yellow eyes steady on Erica. It had taken Erica and Nimue a long time to get used to each other. In fact, they were still getting used to each other. But Erica couldn't deny the warrior was a fierce fighter. Though, fortunately, with Erica still in training, none of them had had to fight much yet.

The second cat, Nestor, was a huge Maine coon with long silver and black fur and very pointed ears. He settled on the ground near Galahad, his eyes glowing yellow in the weak winter light coming in through the living room's open curtains. She'd gotten along better with Nestor on first meeting, but Nestor was older than any of the other cat-warriors she'd met, and she suspected he'd been assigned to her because he was amiable and easy going, but also extremely experienced in the whole realm war, guardian, protect existence thing.

Erica, on the other hand, was not. She'd only learned this was her destiny in October. And she was still adjusting to it all.

"Jilly's timing is horrible," she said as she dropped her oversized purse next to the coffee table and slipped out of her coat. She flung the coat over the arm of her overstuffed couch just to watch Galahad's eye twitch. He was an extremely organized person. Everything had a place and should be put in that place, in his world view. For reasons she refused to think about too closely, but that had something to do with her aunt and his father's relationship, she liked ruffling Galahad's composure. Even just a little bit.

With things like not hanging her coat in the closet by the door.

"I have a meeting with my department head tomorrow. I have to prepare for that."

The other things, getting ahead on her lectures, the research project, were things she could technically put off for a few days if necessary. She'd had to learn how to be flexible between her regular life and this new…destined life. She tried hard not to resent that flexibility or the need to change plans at the last minute. Her destiny involved preventing a war that would destroy her realm, so that really did have to take precedence. But keeping up the pretense between both lives was exhausting.

And it made keeping her job and all that entailed more difficult. Which sucked. Because she loved her job. She'd wanted to be a historian since learning that was a possible job at eight. She *liked* the work and research she did.

But she did also want the world to keep spinning and wasn't particularly eager for the Wraith-Elder war to get going again. So she'd accepted her destiny. And made room for it.

Destiny's timing kind of sucked, though.

Her aunt's timing wasn't the best either.

"This isn't a training session," Galahad said. "This is… something else."

She straightened her shoulders, glanced at her other cats, then at Galahad. "Spit it out. What's the 'something'?"

"There's a book we need to retrieve. Jilly's finally found it. And there's not a lot of time to waste."

An adventure to retrieve a book. Not just read them. Not just learning how her destined job worked. Actually *doing* the job?

"Why didn't you say so in the first place?"

She hurried to her bedroom and retrieved the sword and scabbard she kept in her closet. It was new. And she hadn't had more than the most basic of training with it yet—the fighting was part of this destiny of hers, but not the most important part so they'd given less initial time to it—but she still brought it with her every time she returned to the temple.

After a quick glance down at her work slacks and button down, long-sleeve silk shirt, she also changed clothes. She liked the shirt and didn't want it ripped. But also, the clothes were very impractical for...well an adventure. She hadn't quite adopted the other-realm clothes yet. Jilly promised to get her "proper leathers" soon, which Erica assumed meant the pants and vest and shirt that all reminded her of a Ren Faire costume. But Erica didn't remind her of that promise. She wasn't sure why. After getting over the drama of it all, the clothes weren't the worst part of this destiny business. She just...

Well, she liked her jeans and t-shirts and switching to the other realm clothes felt like more of a commitment, maybe? Like once she started wearing the uniform, there was no going back?

Anyway, none of that mattered at the moment. She slipped into her jeans and a plain cream-colored t-shirt—she'd learned early on that if anything had patterns or logo or anything on it, that could cause weird interactions with some of the books in the temple. Then she slipped on a solid blue flannel shirt. The temple realm wasn't cold like winter in Chicago. No need for her coat. But it was still cooler there now than it had been when she'd first been introduced to the place, so the extra shirt was needed.

By the time she got back out to the living room, strapping her scabbard belt around her waist, the other two cats were already gone.

"Ready?" Galahad asked, his gaze jumping away from her when she looked up.

"Ready."

She followed him to the central post in the cat tree, a thick, cylindrical piece that was large enough to looked more like an actual tree trunk if not for the flat, blue carpet covering it. Galahad went through first, stepping into the central post, into the portal that led to the temple realm. Watching him disappear *into* the cat tree never cease to unnerve her. Even after months, Erica hadn't quite gotten used walking *into* her cat tree and ending up in a completely different realm.

Glancing back at the books stacked on her coffee table, she sighed. Maybe she could reschedule tomorrow's meeting. She wasn't getting any prep done tonight.

She faced the tree again, and a little smile crept out. As far as excuses went, an adventure to retrieve a sacred book was a pretty excellent one.

Erica took a deep breath, preparing for the low-level nausea, and stepped into the cat tree.

CHAPTER TWO

The temple realm was not like Erica's real world in some very fundamental ways. The giant spruce trees, with trunks the size of small buildings, she might almost have been able to imagine in her own realm. There were places in the US with trees that were almost this large. It was conceivable. Even the oversized ferns, with individual fronds that rivaled bicycles could almost be believed. The sky was bright blue and cloudless. The air smelled of pine and cedar.

Almost enough to fool the senses.

But then a giant butterfly flipped past, the creature larger than her head. Or the huge birds that looked nothing like a bird in her realm, with their neon feathers and long beaks, glided overhead, their shadow rolling over for much longer than they should have.

And it was obvious they weren't in Illinois anymore.

Even more than the outsized flora and fauna, though, the temple realm *felt* different. There was a sort of charge in the air, a buzz that felt like static against her skin. Not bad. She was actually starting to like that sensation. But it was obviously not the same as being at home.

She stood still for a long moment to let the nausea pass. She hadn't thrown up in more than a month after the transit, but she didn't want to push her luck. Fortunately, there'd been a few hours since her last meal so the nausea settled quickly.

Galahad stood in the middle of the path to the temple, looking just as he had in her living room and yet somehow larger here. Like this was where he *actually* belonged.

Which, she supposed, in some ways, he did.

Two more people moved out of the trees behind him. One man was tall enough to tower over Galahad. His thick hair, beard, and mustache all blended together into one well-tended mass of dark gray and black. There were braids in his hair, running down the side of his temples. And his green eyes were bracketed by faint lines in skin the color of the spruce tree trunks. He also wore a set of "leathers", the trousers well-worn gray leather, his thick leather vest dotted with metal spikes.

Nestor looked a lot fiercer and scarier in his human form. But somehow, she still felt very comfortable with him. The man had a way of exuding calming energy that Erica found she needed these days. He winked at her before turning down the path.

The woman on the other side of Galahad gave Erica a slight nod before following Nestor. Nimue wasn't as tall as Galahad or even Aunt Jilly, closer to Erica's height. Her hair in this form was also short, loosely cut into a pixie style with tufts of brown and white throughout. Her skin was pale and her eyes brown. Her leathers soft blacks and blues.

While they were still dancing around each other, getting comfortable in each other's presence, Nimue was also deferential to Erica in this realm. Something that…bothered

Erica for reasons she couldn't exactly pinpoint. She really didn't want deference. From any of them. That felt awkward and unearned. At this point, she'd just settle for comfortable.

She followed Nestor and Nimue, Galahad falling in beside her. Speaking of not quite comfortable...

The walk to the temple was a lot less anxiety filled compared to her first trip here, when the Wraith-sworn had been circling and things were teetering on an edge she hadn't understood. This time, the walk to the temple was pleasant in the bright sunshine and warm, pine-scented air. Though, walking beside Galahad like this always left her...edgy.

And since she refused to acknowledge *why* she felt edgy, she turned to conversation. "Do I have to wait until the temple, or can you tell me what this book is we're going to be looking for?"

"Jilly can explain better," Galahad said, without looking down at her.

She refused to shiver at the sound of his rumbling voice. It wasn't cold here. She had no excuse for a shiver. "But you're supposed to be my librarian. Right? So you know what it is we'll be going after?"

She glanced sideways at him in time to see his jaw muscle flex.

Though they were going to be working together for—as far as she could tell—the rest of their lives, and though they were—in a technical, roommate-like sense—living together, and while he did spend more time in this human form now that he could in her realm, they were still not entirely comfortable with each other. He was one of her main trainers, along with her Aunt Jilly and Galahad's father, Memnon. And his father and her aunt had a relationship that went well past work.

But until Jilly had summarily informed Erica that this

guardian business was her destiny, that Erica would inherit the job from her aunt as Jillian had inherited the job from her aunt, and her aunt from another family member before that, until all that had come to light, Erica had only known Galahad as a standoffish cat that avoided her every time she came to visit her aunt. The idea that he was more, that he was *this*, and that all her cats were more...aware of human life than the average cat, was something she really hadn't gotten used to yet.

Except for Galahad, though, the others couldn't be anything but cats in her realm. And the only reason Galahad could take this form in her realm now was because she was the guardian in training and he was her personal bodyguard and librarian.

It was all a little complicated and a lot to adapt to in only a few months.

The parts where she was learning to read ancient text that were nothing like anything she'd see in an Earth library, not in any language she'd ever learned, the kinds of books filled with magic, that were magic themselves... That was the cool part of the job. She hadn't worked up the courage to looking at the brain melting books yet. But that was okay. She wasn't in a hurry to get to those. Since, apparently, the language would literally cook a human brain.

She also enjoyed learning to use the sword hanging on her hip, at least the fundamentals, so that it was more than just a decorative key. She especially liked training with Memnon. Because even though she'd only just discovered the truth a few months ago, she found herself starting to think of Memnon like an uncle pretty quickly. He was patient with her. And there was no weird, awkward tension.

Like there was with Galahad.

"It's still better that Jilly explains," Galahad said. "This is more...her purview."

"If you say so. One day, you're going to have to get past this keeping information to yourself thing, though."

That muscle in his jaw flexed again.

Nimue and Nestor studiously kept their attention focused on the path ahead, pretending to ignore the conversation they were very keenly listening to. They might be in human form here, but Erica knew they were no less curious than they were in cat form.

She stopped grilling Galahad and just enjoyed the rest of the walk, that slight static buzz of electricity on her skin filling her with a kind of energy she didn't have when she was in her own realm. She felt...bigger here. More capable. More...physical? Which was a weird thing since, so far, the majority of her training had involved just reading.

They broke through the huge trees, into a clearing, and the temple rose before them. A giant golden pyramid. In the middle of a spruce and redwood forest.

Made of tan sandstone that reflected light to make the temple look like actual gold, it was built of huge stacked stones that rose like rough steps to a flat top stone. The bottom layer of stones was easily seven foot tall, so there was no way to climb the "stairs" made by the rising layers. But until standing right next to the temple, the illusion that she could climb the outside to the top always caught her.

The entrance was a dark hole in one of the bottom stones, surrounded by smaller bricks with carvings in one of the most sacred languages that existed in the multi-realms—one she still couldn't read—and beside the entrance, two tall, stylized stone cats sat guard, their tails wrapped around their legs. The statues were slightly recessed and as tall as the base stones, and each had an elaborate neckpiece carved around their necks and chests.

She'd never gotten a really long, good look at the cat statues guarding the temple entrance because every time she came here, Galahad seemed to be in a hurry to get inside and get to work. But one day, she was going to stand in this clearing and study those statues. She had a feeling there was something to the neckpieces that was important.

But not this time. This time, they had things to do. More than just the training. Her stomach danced a little. The last technical adventure involved running away from Wraithsworn and the near breach of the temple. She was sort of hoping for a less deadly adventure this time. But anything that wasn't just endless training still sounded exciting.

Nimue and Nestor had fanned out to either side of the temple entrance, looking almost like the human versions of the guardian cat statues behind them. Erica walked past them, with Galahad just behind her, into the dark maw of the entrance. Which was really just a short tunnel that led down to a large wooden door.

At the door, Erica pulled her sword. Jilly had patiently taught her the words required to open the temple, and shown her exactly how to hold the sword in front of a row of glyphs, so that the key glyphs hidden in the metal of her sword would open the lock glyphs beside the door. It had taken her a few practice runs to be able to open the door successfully, though.

Eventually, she'd inherit the real sword, Alendrial, once she became the temple guardian. Right now, while Alendrial still belonged to Jilly, Erica used a sort of…trainer sword. One that could help her open the temple, and even light the interior if needs be. But it didn't glow with the same blue light as Alendrial. And it didn't talk to her the way Alendrial apparently did with Jilly. Her aunt promised her that one day the sword would start speaking to her, when the sword—and Erica—were ready.

She wouldn't inherit Alendrial until Jilly stopped being the guardian. And as far as Erica could tell, that happened when Jilly died. Since Erica wasn't in a hurry for her aunt to pass away, she could wait on Alendrial for as long as that took.

Until then, Erica used the non-sentient starter sword.

She held the long length of metal up in front of the glyphs and took a deep breath. This part had felt incredibly awkward at first. And getting the words right to activate everything had taken her an embarrassingly long time. But now she was comfortable opening the temple without Jilly standing right beside her to help.

Still, she got a little twist in her gut every time, worried she'd screw it all up *this* time and not be able to get the door open. And that would be really embarrassing in front of her guardian cats. Especially Galahad.

Fortunately, this was not that embarrassing day. The door hissed open with a release of sandalwood-scented air that never ceased to make Erica sigh.

Unlike her first visit, the inside of the temple was already alight. Like that first visit, Erica stood at the entrance and glanced around the interior of the pyramid in awe.

Wall to wall books. There were no rooms. Just a giant, open space filled with books. Galleries above her circled the exterior wall, getting smaller as they rose toward the top of the huge pyramid, each lined with shelves and stacks and tables full of books. The rug-covered main floor of the pyramid was overwhelmed by books too. Everything from standard hardbacks wrapped in leather, to papyrus scrolls capped with copper seals, to stone and clay tablets. Stacked on tables, piled on the floor, squeezed into free standing shelves and the shelves that lined the walls.

A golden glow of some of the most incredible and precious books the realms had to offer.

Jilly stepped out from behind the half wall that blocked much of the ground floor from the temple entrance, pulling Erica from her appreciation of the sheer wonder of the room.

"About time you got here," Jilly said, as she waved Erica deeper into the temple. "Hurry. We don't have time to waste."

Erica's heart started to thump. The last time Jilly had said that to her…

The Wraith-sworn had nearly broken into the temple.

CHAPTER THREE

Erica's Aunt Jilly was a six-foot-tall woman in her early sixties, her gray-blond hair currently pulled back into a complicated braid wrapped up in a bun, and wearing her well-worn brown leather pants, boots and a loose cream top. Her sword, Alendrial, was in a scabbard attached to a belt around Jilly's hips. And though Jilly was only about two inches taller than Erica, in this realm she looked larger than life. A woman who fit here in this place of magic and shapeshifting warriors.

For most of Erica's life, Jilly had just been the cool aunt, the one her mother and other aunt bemoaned for never getting married and having kids. The aunt who cursed and did crafting and went on a lot of trips and owned a whole bunch of cats.

It wasn't until October that Erica had learned the truth.

Jilly was actually the guardian of this temple, though she didn't like the word "guardian" for the job. And she went around retrieving vital texts from different realms to store here so that neither the Wraiths—entities not unlike the Wraiths of myth on Earth, ghost-like creatures of immense power—nor the Elders—entities similar to old gods on Earth and equally powerful—could get those texts and restart a war that had been going on since time immemorial. A war that would destroy all the realms, including Erica's.

No one was sure why Erica's family had been tapped for the responsibility of guarding the temple. The job passed around to the various entities in all the different realms. But for the last few centuries, that responsibility was her realms' and more specifically, her family's.

And soon, it would be Erica's.

"What's happening, Jilly?" Erica followed her aunt into the temple.

Here rugs covered large chunks of the wooden floor, a few chairs scattered around between the piles and stacks of books, and even some cushions scattered over the floor. The sheer number of books became more obvious, too. There was a catalogue list somewhere around here, recording every book in the temple. It was a very long list.

Jilly's own librarian, bodyguard cat, and romantic partner, Memnon, waited near a table in the center of the temple's large ground floor. Erica jogged to keep up with her aunt as they joined him.

"Good to see you, Erica," Memnon said in his deep rumbling voice, smiling softly before turning a more intense look on his son.

Galahad and Memnon were obviously related, both with dark black hair and blue eyes, though Memnon had streaks of white in his hair and lines bracketing his eyes and forming a ridge between his brows. Memnon wasn't as tall as his son, either. In fact, he was closer to Erica's height, a little shorter than Jilly, and a bit wider than Galahad. But even with the differences, there was no mistaking Memnon was Galahad's sire.

The intense look between father and son sparked Erica's curiosity, but she reined in her questions when Jilly gestured to the book sitting on the reading table in front of Memnon.

"I thought we had to *retrieve* a book?" Erica asked, coming to stand beside her aunt and pulling off her flannel shirt in the much warmer temple interior. She started to drop it under the table, but Galahad took it from her and draped it neatly over a chair. She didn't not grin. Even though she was tempted.

"We do have to retrieve a book," Jilly said, ignoring the interaction. "The information about it is in this book. Read this passage. Then we'll go."

Frowning, but having learned it's usually best not to waste time asking and to just do as Jilly asks when she was in a hurry, Erica looked down at the book.

It wasn't as large or elaborate as some of the books in the temple. This one was actually quite small, a little bigger than her hands, hardbacked with a casing that was almost like cardboard, covered in little scratch marks that, if she stared at them long enough, resolved into a sort of language similar to maybe Ogham or Runic markings. A lot of lines and slashes that translated to language in her mind.

Many of the books in the library did that for her. And only for her and Jilly. Maybe Memnon, and now Galahad—neither of them would say yes or no when she asked. But definitely for her and for Jilly. The odd markings that didn't look like words or language would…shift and arrange themselves—either actually or just in her mind, depending on the book—until she could read the text. She still had to learn a lot of new languages to read many of the books here. But unlike historians of old, if there was an ancient or forgotten language here, and she needed to read that book, she didn't need a

Rosetta Stone to translate it. The book translated itself for her.

Which was actually really cool.

This one did that, though it didn't look like much of a magical book on the surface. The cardboard cover was an ordinary tan color even. There was no gold leafing or jewels or elaborate drawings. Just the scratch marks, the cardboard, and some relatively plain cream paper inside. There did seem to be a few little nicks in the pages, like something sharp had caught them and dug little holes or taken tiny slices from the edge of a page. But none of that seemed to interfere with the writing on the inside of the book.

Or else the writing had rearranged itself to move around the nicks. Hard to tell with books inside the temple.

The cover scratch marks had given her a title: *Beware the Shiny Objects That Distract*.

Weird title. Good advice, she supposed. Probably something was lost in translation. That was the other thing about the books that rearranged themselves so she could read them—occasionally, the stories couldn't translate well into her language. And that's where a lot of interpretation came in.

She didn't bother asking what page to open to. The moment she flipped the book open, it landed on a page about a third of the way in. An image on one side, a rough pencil—or pencil-like—sketch of what she'd swear was a little jingle bell. Small and round with a little X opening in the base. The text on the opposite page was just more scratches for a moment, so she stared hard until the paragraph resolved.

"'The worst of the worst,'" she read under her breath. "'The sounds will drive a mind into distraction and humors no living being should experience until the time of the great dying and all is lost.'" She made a face. This was definitely one of those books that didn't translate well. She looked up at Jilly and raised a brow in questions.

Jilly just nodded back to the book. "Keep going."

Erica sighed. A simple explanation would be a lot faster. She continued reading aloud. "'Dangerous and funny. Like weeds. Take heed, unwary. For this bell jingles death. It is planted amidst the boxes for safety. Do not sit. Do not sleep. Though you will be tempted. The book will set you free.'"

Erica closed her eyes for a moment, letting the after image of the lines forming into words fade. Then she opened her eyes and looked at Jilly again. "This makes no sense. It's a joke? What book are we after?"

"The...protections, for lack of a better word, on the book we're hunting are substantial. But odd. I'm still not entirely sure what the passage means. That's why I wanted you to read it too. This is the first time we've had a clue where to look for this particular artifact, and the warnings around it are cryptic enough, I thought we'd better make this a team effort."

"Okay. Sounds...good? I guess."

"Just remember what you've read. The key to solving everything lies in those words. We just won't be sure how until we get there."

"And where, exactly, is there?"

"Follow me. Time to learn about the temple tree."

Jilly pointed to the giant cat tree filling in one corner of the temple. It was huge. Larger than the one in Jilly's bedroom. Definitely larger than Erica's. When she'd first seen this tree, the padding and scratch material and carpeting covering the various platforms and levels and thick trunks had been a dark cobalt blue. The next time she'd visited the temple, the color was a lighter blue color, closer to turquoise, and Erica had just assumed her memory of the thing had been off. After all, that first time had been pretty intense.

But then the tree changed colors again. To a navy blue so dark it was nearly black. And after that, it appeared as a very ordinary blue, a color that in a crayon box would just be called "blue." The time after that, a pale color close to white with just a hint of blue. And the time after that an intense color with purples and yellows in the background that reminded Erica a little too much of a bruise.

No one had commented on the changing color. And no one had explained it to her. Jilly had told her she wasn't ready for that particular tree yet, so she'd made note of the changing colors and curbed her curiosity. Given some of the books in here melted brains—which wasn't nearly as funny a fact as Jilly seemed to think it was—when Jilly told her she wasn't ready for something, Erica believed her. Especially since the other cat trees in Erica's life were portals.

Today, the temple tree was a shade of blue that was nearly green. Looked at from one angle, definitely green, another more blue. As they neared the giant structure, more people walked out from the stacks, appearing from behind shelves, and forming up around Jilly like they'd been there all along.

These were Jilly's guards. Five of them in total. Six if counting Memnon. Between Erica's small contingent of three and Jilly's six, there were a lot of guardians to protect the two...guardians.

Erica was starting to get Jilly's point about the word "guardian" not being a great one when describing what she and Jilly did here.

At one time, Galahad had been among Jilly's guards. But now he was one of Erica's. She glanced back. He was right where he always was when they left her realm. Just behind her right shoulder. Keeping watch over her. It was both reassuring and occasionally annoying. Right now, as they stepped up to the giant temple tree, Erica found his presence extremely comforting.

Actually, the presence of all of the guards was comforting. Having all of them there, with their swords and fighting skills, as she embarked on her first retrieval was enough to shore up her suddenly jumping nerves.

She pressed a hand to her stomach and looked up at the top of the temple cat tree, which was several feet over her head. None of the guards, when in their cat forms, every jumped up on this tree, or napped on the platforms or inside the hide boxes. She was about to find out why.

"It'll be fine," Galahad said in a whisper, leaning in close to speak near her ear. "We've got your back."

"Thank you," she whispered back, smiling up at him.

Then blinked hard and focused forward again. Stomach still jumping, heart still pounding. Had to just be fear. That was her story and she was sticking to it.

Jilly turned to her, her hand resting on the hilt of her sword in its scabbard. "This transition won't be like the ones you're used to. We won't just be stepping through into another place. This is…more of a journey. Every time we use this portal, we're going somewhere new. So the trip is always disorienting. You'll get used to that, too, eventually. This first time, don't panic. We're all with you, and you'll be fine." She smiled. "I'm still here, right? If I can do this, so can you. You were meant to."

"Not a single bit of this sounds good or reassuring, Aunt Jilly."

Jilly chuckled. "You'll understand on the other side. Just remember not to panic. We've got you."

"Are we walking into something dangerous?"

"Always." Jilly winked and turned back toward the tree.

Yeah, that wink wasn't reassuring either. But the thought of the adventure ahead overrode Erica's growing panic. She pulled in a deep breath. She could do this.

Jilly and Memnon approached a post in the tree, not the central one, but one of the thick side "branches." In both her tree and Jilly's, the central post, the thickest post, was the one that served as the doorway between realms. Realizing that more than one post on this tree would go to a different place was…scary.

No wonder no one got too close.

"Ready?" Jilly asked.

Which was unusual for Jilly. She didn't normally wait on Erica to be ready, just launched into things. That had Erica's heartbeat pounding hard again.

"Ready," she said. And even though she was nervous, she really was ready. This was exciting and terrifying and what she'd been training for for months.

She was ready.

CHAPTER FOUR

She had not been ready. Not even a little bit.

Just as Jilly had warned her, this transition from one realm to another hadn't been like walking through a door, a little light and darkness and disorientation and then out into a new realm. No, this had involved moving lights, and a lot of time, and the sense of her atoms being split apart and reformed as she flew through a tunnel that twisted and turned and worse...every so often it paused.

Those pauses had been terrifying. Just hanging in the middle of a blackness, not able to see or hear. The only thing she'd felt was her own panic rising, an existential terror that far outweighed anything she'd felt up to that moment.

She'd been afraid she'd died in the transit. Each pause, she was certain she'd died.

And then with a breath stealing suddenness—was she even breathing? She couldn't tell—the movement would start again and she'd be flung through a tunnel of bright white lights, until finally...

They stepped into a new world.

And Erica didn't even have a moment to look around before she turned and threw up.

Bent over, hands on her knees, eyes closed, she rethought all her life choices. Including what she'd had for lunch.

A gentle hand rubbed her back, up by her shoulders, and she realized someone was holding her hair back, keeping her loose braid from falling forward while she retched. She straightened, thinking she'd see Jilly at her back, only to realize it was Galahad.

She wanted to be embarrassed that he'd just seen her throw up, but she was too caught on the fact that he'd held her hair out of the way. Also, this wasn't the first time he'd seen her barf after a transition.

"Okay?" he asked quietly.

"Was I the only one who threw up?" she whispered.

"Nimue did too, if that helps."

"She did?" Erica wasn't sure why she was surprised by that. She just assumed all the cat-guards were experts at this transitioning stuff.

"She hasn't gone through the temple tree very often. She's almost as new to this as you are."

And Erica had had no idea. Damn.

Though…did that change anything? She felt like she might have made more progress on her relationship with Nimue if she'd known. This newness gave them something to bond over. Then again, Nimue might not have wanted Erica to know she was new to this.

It was something they probably should talk about when all this was done, though.

Until then, Erica filed the information away. "Is she okay?"

"She's fine. Nestor has her. She's already back to her human form."

"The transition made her go cat again?"

"Coming out here threw her body back to cat. But not for long."

"Are there other realms you all can't be human in? Like my realm. Except for you now, of course."

"There are. This isn't one of them."

"What happens if we have to retrieve a book from one of those realms?"

"We still protect the guardian. We just do it as cats instead of carrying swords."

"And that...works?"

Galahad's mouth ticked up at one corner, an amused smile he looked like he was trying to suppress. "You ever seen a real and proper cat fight before?"

"No. Not sure I want to."

"We're just as good bodyguards in our cat form. Don't worry. You're always safe with us."

Yeah. She'd suspected as much.

She did feel safer with her cat-guards. Even knowing Nimue was new didn't diminish her faith in them. She was more surprised that she felt that way on instinct than she was surprised at the feeling itself.

"What now?" She looked around, dragging her gaze from Galahad finally.

Erica gasped quietly at her first view of a brand new—to her—realm. Unlike the temple realm, they hadn't stepped out into a forest, and they hadn't stepped out into the middle of a city either. They were standing under a tall palm that seemed to be the only tree in a great expanse of rolling desert hills. Sand dunes. Nothing but pinkish orange sand dunes as far as Erica could see.

A lot of sand. One lone palm tree. And a lot of bright yellow sunshine.

The heat from the sun rose off the sands in simmering waves, creating clear whirling eddies over the dunes. The air under the palm tree—which was larger than any palm tree she'd ever seen in her life, its trunk about four times thicker than a typical Earth palm—was cool enough to be comfortable. But the heat looked intimidating out from under the thick fronds.

"Did we think to bring water?" Erica asked in a small voice. There was a *lot* of desert out there.

"Everyone recovered?" Jilly asked, clapping her hands together like an overeager tour guide trying to get the attention of her group.

Erica raised her hand, a kid in school trying to Jilly's attention. "Did we bring water?"

"We won't be here long enough to need it."

Erica stared at the desert dubiously.

Jilly opened her mouth to say more, but stopped when all nine of the cat-guards, including Memnon and Galahad turned in one direction at the exact same time.

Erica exchanged a frown with Jilly, then turned to her three guards, one at a time. Nester frowned through the bush of his beard. Nimue was practically bouncing on her toes as she stared into the desert. Galahad, though, looked fierce, intent. Like he was about to charge into battle. This wasn't the first time she'd seen him like this, but it was the first time she hadn't been able to even sense the problem. He had his hands at his sides, though, clenched into fists, rather than having a hand on his sword.

And that was the part that really struck her. As she looked around at all the cat-guards, every single one of them staring in the exact same direction with varying degrees of intensity in their expression, not a single one of them had reached for their weapons.

"Uhm…" She raised her brows at Jilly.

Jilly shrugged.

"Helpful," she muttered under her breath, then followed the cat-guards' gazes, looking out over the desert.

She couldn't see anything. Just soft rolling sand dunes and bright yellow sunshine. No trees. No people. Nothing shimmered in the distance like a mirage—which actually was a little weird given the heat. No sandstorms darkening the sky in the distance.

She stepped closer to the edge of the palm tree's shade, squinting in an attempt to see into the distance farther. She didn't have the cats' senses. Maybe there was something there just too small or far away for her to see.

Galahad shot a hand out and grabbed her arm, pulling her abruptly back from the sunlight.

"What? What?" Panic bubbled up. What was out there that had all the cats so freaked out? Freaked out enough, Galahad hadn't wanted her to go too far away. And really, she'd only been steps from him.

"Something…" His voice was quiet, hesitant. "Can you hear it? Like a jingling sound…"

Erica looked at Jilly again. To see Memnon standing in front of her. None of the cats had pulled their swords yet, but Jilly had hers out now.

Yeah. Yeah, that seemed smart. Erica was tempted to pull her own sword out. Except that she wasn't very good with it yet. There hadn't been time. She could barely do that parrying thing. She was almost certain she couldn't fight with the sword yet. She'd have to rely on the cat-guards.

"Where's the book we're here to get?" she murmured to Jilly. If it was in the same direction the cats were staring, that would be…significant.

Jilly gave her a look that said everything, but she still

nodded in the direction the cats were staring. "It's supposed to be buried in the sand. There are markers, magical ones. I was going to show you how to find and follow them, but..."

"Doesn't look like we'll need that," Erica finished, glancing at the guards. To Galahad, she said, "Is there a reason we're not heading that way? Why are we just standing here?"

"Can't you hear it? That bell sound? The jingling... It's... It sets my teeth on edge."

That couldn't be good.

Erica barely had time to register what Galahad was saying when suddenly a large calico cat took off across the sands.

"Nimue!" Nester called and suddenly there was a huge, silver Maine Coon racing after the calico.

Chaos erupted then as all Jilly's cats but Memnon transformed to their cat shapes and chased after the others. Galahad held his human shape too, and he didn't loosen his hold on Erica's arm.

"We have to follow them," she said, looking up at Galahad. "Come on!"

Jilly was already moving around Memnon to follow as well.

"Wait!" Galahad tightened his hold Erica's arm. "There's something out there. Something dangerous. I can feel it in the sand."

"A worm? A dragon?" Jilly asked.

Erica eeped. Dragons? They didn't warn her there could be dragons here. Worms sounded not too bad. Except...this was a strange realm and that meant she couldn't assume when Jilly said worms that meant the little ones she was used to at home.

"How big should I expect a worm to be here?" she asked.

"Big," Jilly said. "Bigger than the sand-dragons."

That's what she'd been afraid of. "How big are the sand-dragons?"

"Big," Jilly said.

"Helpful," Erica said. Again. "Could have warned me."

"Didn't expect them this time of year. That's why we came now."

"This isn't worms or sand-dragons," Memnon said.

"It's something else," Galahad added. "That sound…"

Erica felt Galahad shiver behind her and turned to look up at him. He was sweating, his jaw tight, and a muscle in his cheek bounced. His grip on her arm was so tight it was starting to hurt.

"You okay?" she asked, lifting a hand to his jaw to try and force his attention to her instead of the distant…whatever it was that was doing this to the cats.

"No," he said. He swallowed, looked down at her.

She blinked and suddenly Galahad's cat stared up at her. He was black and silky in this form, with white patches on his chest and back. His long black tail twitched twice. Then he turned and raced out over the sands.

"Damn it," Memnon said, and then another black cat raced after Galahad.

Erica exchanged another look with Jilly. Jilly squared her shoulders. And they both took off into the open sand, chasing after the cats.

CHAPTER FIVE

The term herding cats was a good and appropriate metaphor for chaos. Erica had never fully appreciated that phrase until she'd gotten cats of her own. Even though, technically, they were cat-humans, and technically, they worked for her. They were still cats. With all the tenacity, stubbornness, and independence that came with the species.

Sometimes, this was great. Erica didn't have to worry about being at work all day, or getting home late, or anything. She didn't have to worry about taking them out for walks or even feeding them since Galahad could go human and get them food if they needed something while she was gone.

But sometimes, that tendency toward stubbornness caused more problems than it solved.

As the desert opened up around Erica, the dunes shifting under her feet, the heat of the yellow sun beating down on her, the dry air and faint salty scent of the sands tickling her nose, she decided this was one of those moments when the cats were definitely causing the problems.

She panted hard, trying to keep up with Jilly's longer

strides, but the loose sand kept changing under her and made moving fast impossible. She fell a couple of times and had to jog to catch up with Jilly. That just kicked up more sand and made the going more difficult.

Her leather boots were tall enough on her calf she wasn't getting sand in her shoes and that was good. But the leather was also not the sort of breathable clothing choice she would have made for this environment.

In the distance, she could still just see the black shapes of Galahad and Memnon tearing over the orange-pink sands, but the other cats had disappeared in the dips and valleys of the dunes.

"Can you hear the jingling Galahad was talking about?" she asked Jilly through her panting attempts to catch her breath. Walking through deep, shifting sand was *hard*. Why had she never realized this before?

"I can't," Jilly said.

And Erica was only a little mollified to realize Jilly was breathing hard, too. Jilly was thirty years older than Erica, and that age difference meant Erica should be more concerned with Jilly's health. But honestly, Erica was more mortified that she was in worse shape than her much older aunt.

"Whatever it is, it's outside our meager human hearing range," Jilly continued. "But a bell sound is interesting."

"Why? What does it mean?"

"Remember the passage in the book?"

Erica pulled the words out of her memory—the one good talent she'd been able to bring to this job was a good memory for things she read. If she saw the words on a page of some kind, she usually recalled them.

Aloud she repeated the full, nonsensical, passage. "'The worst of the worst. The sounds will drive a mind into distraction and humors no living being should experience until the time of the great dying and all is lost. Dangerous and funny. Like weeds. Take heed, unwary. For this bell jingles death.'" She stopped abruptly at that line, her eyes widening. "Shit."

Jilly glanced back. "Indeed."

They lurched over another dune, clearing the top in time to see Galahad, Memnon close on his tail, disappearing behind another rise.

"Damn it," Jilly muttered, and slid-ran down the slippery sands into the next valley.

Erica followed, her heart pounding as panic made her limbs unsteady. Sweat dripped down her back, making cotton t-shirt stick to her skin. There wasn't a whiff of air movement to cool her sweat either. The sun pounded against her unprotected head—should have brought a hat—and the glare off the sands made her squint. The only chance they had of catching up with the cats was if the cats stopped. Her and Jilly's two human legs just weren't moving over the sands fast enough to keep up with the fleet-footed cats.

She was panting as much from worry and exertion by the time they cleared the next dune. And she nearly plowed into Jilly's back because she'd been more focused on keeping her footing than looking where she was going. After all, what was she going to bump into in the middle of all this sand? It wasn't like there were tree branches to bean herself on.

Which was why Jilly's abrupt stop just in front of her caught her out and she had to backpedal to keep from sliding down the back of the dune again. When she regained her balance, she followed Jilly's gaze into the next valley.

"Uh oh," she muttered. "This isn't good."

"No," Jilly said. "No, it is not."

Below them, half-buried in the sands, sat what looked to

be a bunch of scattered cardboard boxes. Though Erica couldn't tell from this distance if they were real cardboard or just that color. The box shapes stuck out of the sand randomly and were a tan brown color that stood out enough from the orange-pink sand to make them obvious, but not so obvious she would have noticed them from any farther distance. In fact, they almost looked like hollowed out stones popping out of the ground. Just extremely square and rectangular shaped stones.

And in the middle of several of those box-shaped things, sat all but two of the nine cats. Folded and fitted to squeeze into the open spaces. Some of them with their eyes closed, obviously asleep. Others still squishing themselves into the boxes. Sitting. And sleeping. And looking extremely comfortable.

Except...

"The passage said not to sit or sleep," she hissed at Jilly. "What the hell are they doing?"

"What cat's everywhere do," Jilly said with a sigh and a curse under her breath. "If they fits, they sits."

"This isn't funny. This is not even close to time for funny."

"Do I sound like I'm laughing?"

Jilly jogged and slid down the hill, fast enough Erica cursed herself and followed, hoping neither of them fell and went head over heels into all those cat-filled boxes.

"Get out!" Jilly shouted at the cats as she reached the boxes. She waved her hands overhead, hissed and shouted, even clucked her tongue.

The cats ignored her.

And since these were supposed to be guardian cats who protected Jilly from all things, this behavior was a lot more disturbing than the usual cats-ignoring-human behavior.

Erica raced toward Galahad and Memnon, the only two not curled up inside boxes. They were facing off, hissing at each other, the hair along their backs raised.

That didn't look good at all.

Galahad, standing next to a box, swiped at Memnon like he was defending the box. Memnon lunged forward and leapt back in a quick move that Erica missed, but Galahad howled.

The howl made Erica want to intervene, but she was afraid to get between father and son. "Galahad!" She slid to a stop near the two cats, dropping into the sand. "Whatever is happening, stop! I need you to go back to human so you can tell me what's happening."

Galahad hissed at Memnon, ignoring her. Memnon swiped at him again and this close, Erica saw his claws were out. There was a little trickle of blood along Memnon's ear. And a spot of blood on Galahad's nose.

Damn it. Was Galahad preventing Memnon from getting in a box or was it the other way around? Galahad had taken off first. Memnon had chased him. But...she just couldn't tell who was trying to save who here? Or if they were just fighting over which one of them got the box at Galahad's back.

The boxes, when Erica was close enough to look at them better, looked even more like ordinary cardboard. They couldn't possibly be. But up close, all she saw was stiff brown cardboard and open flaps folded back and held down by the surrounding sands. What the hell were boxes doing in the middle of all this desert?

Another hiss from Memnon and he lunged at Galahad again. Galahad was half turned toward the box behind him. Didn't see the attack coming. Memnon got a hold of his neck and jerked, tugging Galahad off his feet.

The move tore a howl of protest from Galahad and he

turned on his father, so suddenly and viciously Erica could hardly believe this was the same Galahad she'd known all these months.

"No! Stop!" She moved as close as she dared as the two cats rolled over each other, hissing and screeching, the flash of sharp claws catching sunlight. "Stop! Galahad. Stop!"

"I can't get them out!" Jilly shouted. "They won't budge from the boxes. Even when I try to lift them. I can't."

"Shit." Erica rolled through a steady stream of profanities under her breath as she looked around. There had to be something they could do.

The book! The passage had said…

"Jilly. The passage said, 'The book will set you free.' That has to be the answer. The book. We have to find it." She started searching around the boxes. "It said it would be 'planted amidst the boxes,' right? It has to be here somewhere."

"There's something growing over them," Jilly said.

"Weeds? There was something like that in the passage, too. Shit. We have to find the book."

Jilly dropped to the ground between the randomly scattered boxes and started hunting through the sands.

"What are we looking for? You said something about markers? What kind of markers?"

Jilly scowled. "The markers were to get us to this location. I didn't expect the cats to get caught in a spell. Once here, we just have to find the damned thing."

Erica cursed again. Panic made her frantic, and she wanted to just start randomly digging, too. But she didn't even know what she was looking for beside it being a book.

"What does it look like? What am I trying to find exactly?"

"There's no image in the records, just a description," Jilly said, still throwing sand around. "Tan leather binding and plain cream paper. Should be some markings on the outside cover, but the records are unclear what the markings are, just that they're in red."

Tan leather with red markings in the middle of orange-pink sand surrounding by tan brown boxes. Yeah. That won't be hard to find.

She glanced back at Galahad and Memnon. They were separated again, but this time Memnon was standing in front of the box and Galahad was lunging and retreating in quick attacks. There seemed to be more blood. Some of it staining the sands.

Another rush of panic through her blood made Erica see spots. Her gut tightened so much she worried she might throw up again. Fortunately, she didn't have anything left to throw up. Just churning acid as she turned back to desperately hunting around the boxes for the book.

"The passage said it was planted among the boxes," she said, her attention on the sand. "Planted. Does that just mean buried or would there be, like, I don't know... A sprout of some kind above it?"

Jilly looked up from the sifting piles she was moving around. "Planted. Yes. Yes! Look for something growing out of the sand. Something like the weeds that are starting to cover the cats."

For the first time, Erica looked closer at the other cats. The one closest to her, one of Jilly's guards, a cat named Odysseus, had two long thin, brownish-gray vines twining through his fur over his back. Jilly looked at the others. All of them had at least one or two of the vines over their backs, across their curled bodies.

After hunting for a moment, Erica spotted Nimue. She had three of the vines crisscrossing over her back as she slept curled into a tight ball of brown, black, and white inside one of the smaller, square boxes. She seemed completely unaware of the vines, but the vines were tight enough to leave distinct marks in her fluffy fur.

In the box next to her, Nester's huge form spilled out of a box that wasn't nearly large enough for him, but somehow, he still managed to squeeze most of his big body down into it. As Erica watched, a second vine crept up from the box, sliding through Nestor's thick silver fur like a snake through grass.

Erica loosed a steady stream of cursing under her breath as she went back to looking for something poking above the sand, something that looked more like a plant or… She wasn't sure. Like the vines maybe? Except something not covering a cat.

The sounds of Memnon and Galahad's fight set her teeth on edge and made her wince and cringe. The panic and fear pulsed under her skin until she felt like she might explode.

"There!" Jilly shouted.

Erica turned to see a very tiny little brown-gray leaf standing up above the sand near the gap between Nester and Odysseus's boxes. She slid into the sand next to the leaf just as Jilly dropped down beside it. They glanced at each other, then both started digging at once, pushing and shoving the soft sand aside.

But the sand was so silky it kept sliding back into the hole, and it took a lot of effort to push down deep enough to reveal more of the stem under the little leaf. They dug around the stem, digging deeper and deeper, the slithering sand glistening as it tried to fall back into the hole, the smell of dust and salt thick around them.

And something else Erica couldn't quite put her finger to. But some musty scent that made her nose twitch like mad.

"Almost there, almost there," Jilly muttered under her breath as the sounds of Galahad and Memnon's fighting got louder, the screeching and cat screams and yowls filling the air.

All that noise, the other cats *had* to be bespelled for them to just sleep through it. Erica winced at a yowl that sounded like pain, but she didn't turn to see who was hurt and how badly. Save the other cats, save everyone.

The only way to do that was find the damned book.

Scrambling through the soft sand, Erica's fingers finally connected with something not sand. Something hard. And... squishy but hard.

"Found it!" She walked her fingers around the thing, looking for the edges, looking for a way to pry it out of the earth. Jilly joined her, pushing away sand and digging over the top of the thing, looking for edges.

They grasped edges on opposite sides of the book at the same time and lifted.

A large book came out of the sand with a slushing sort of pop, the top still covered with sand.

The sand slid gently off, back into the hole, like a cracked hourglass.

And they were running out of time.

CHAPTER SIX

Jilly took the big book from Erica and dumped off the rest of the soft orange sand before righting it again. And Erica got her first good look at the thing they'd come to retrieve.

She hadn't seen many—any?—round books in her life. Not outside of the books for toddlers and babies. In her mind, book equaled rectangle or square. Or moved into the realm of scroll. Circle wasn't something she instinctively thought of as "book."

She was really going to have to expand her thinking.

The book was covered in the soft pale tan leather, as Jilly had described, with thick stitches of the same kind of leather running only one edge of the circular shape to form a bound side. The top cover had four long, ragged slash marks through the leather. And under that was a kind of reddish color. The whole thing gave the effect of looking like an animal had slashed through actual flesh and there was blood beneath. It was…disturbing to say the least.

As Jilly set the book on the ground, she glanced at the cats. "Damn it, damn it. Memnon!" She started to rise.

Erica grabbed her hand. "Book first. Break whatever spell they're under. Then we'll take care of them. All of them."

Jilly glanced at the fighting cats again, then shook her head and looked back down at the book. "I'm supposed to be the experienced one here."

"And the man you love is fighting his own son to keep his son from succumbing to this spell. Makes sense you'd be distracted."

"You are wise beyond your years, my lovely niece."

"And I'm scared beyond my gut acid, my lovely aunt. Read the book so we can figure out how to fix all this."

Despite the situation, Jilly chuckled under her breath. She slowly, carefully lifted one side of the round cover, easing it open as the binding ties at one side first resisted then slowly gave in to the movement. It was like opening a spiral notebook once the binding loosened, and Jilly was able to lay it flat in the soft sand.

The inside was made of cream paper, like Jilly had said. The writing on the paper, however, wasn't nearly as plain. Some sort of silvery-gold ink had been used. It sparkled in the sunlight. Almost impossible to see thanks to all the reflections and glittering, like light bouncing off metal. Jilly lifted one page, she and Erica both squinting at the writing.

A jingling sound rose up out of the book. A sound like toy bells.

The cat fight behind Erica stopped abruptly. The silence was ominous.

Jilly cursed under her breath but didn't look away from the book. Erica had less restraint. She glanced back. Memnon and Galahad were both staring at her and Jilly. Or more precisely, they were both staring at the book. Their so-similar blue eyes glittered under the sun's glare, their pupils contracted to almost nothing. The stare was intent, focused, and all the fur along both their backs stood up.

Not good. This couldn't be good. "This isn't good."

"I know. I know. Help me. This fucking ink is impossible to seen in the sun."

Erica looked around for something that could serve as a shade, glanced down at her t-shirt and sighed. She should have remembered her flannel shirt, still back at the temple. Ah well. Was too hot for flannel anyway. She had a nice bra on. And everyone was cats right now. What the hell.

She pulled her t-shirt off and draped it over her and Jilly's bent heads. The cream-colored cotton still let through lots of light, but the shade was enough to make the ink on the round pages visible.

"Efficient," Jilly murmured, turning another page.

"Gets the job done, right?" For some reason, Erica wanted to laugh. A laugh that felt out of place in the circumstances.

Hot air brushed her back, cooling her sweat even as the hot sunshine baked her skin. Her Chicago-living, still-deep-in-winter skin. Sun screen on her entire body might have to become part of her routine if she was going to randomly land into deserts like this.

Another giggle bubbled up in her throat as she stared down at the metallic ink. What was she laughing at? There was nothing on the page that should have spurred giggles. In fact, she couldn't read the language on the page at all. It was a series of lines and cuts and the occasional circle. It reminded her of one of the similar styles of writing on Earth like Ogham or Runic. Like the book in the temple containing the passage about this book. Except, unlike the book in the temple, she couldn't seem to make these simple symbols resolve into something she could read.

"I can't read it," she said, keeping most of her attention

on the pages. "Can you? It's not resolving for me." A laughed burst out. She frowned. "I have no idea why I just laughed. I almost giggled earlier. This is not a funny situation. Why do I keep trying to laugh? Nervous tic?"

She had a friend who sometimes laughed at inopportune moments, like if someone fell, not because she found the situation funny but because it was a sort of release of energy from her nervous system. Cali was also one of the first people to jump in and help someone who'd fallen, but people who didn't know her often thought her nervous laughter was rude because they misinterpreted its reason.

This wasn't that. Erica didn't have a nervous laugh tic. There was nothing happening that had any humor to it at all.

Another giggle burst from her.

She widened her eyes at Jilly. "Shit. This can't be good. Do you want to laugh?"

"Holding it in," Jilly said, pressing her lips together hard enough for white lines to bracket her mouth. "It's the book. Part of the passage. Remember?"

Erica ran through the passage in her head again. Got to the relevant part. "'Humors no living being should experience until the time of the great dying'? That sound bad, Jilly. Very bad. Not funny at all."

"Nope." She flipped another page. And a soft giggle escaped her.

Shit. Erica blinked hard, trying to refocus and see the words on the page. "'The book will set you free.' That's what the passage said. Somewhere in here has to be the answer."

Jilly started running her finger over the metallic ink. She hissed in a breath, and Erica was appalled to see blood dripping from Jilly's fingertip. Jilly held her hand out over the sands, letting the little drops of blood fall into the dirt before any could land on the book.

"Rooky mistake," she muttered. Louder, she said, "If it looks metallic, assume it cuts like metal. Don't forget that lesson the way I just did."

"All metallic ink will cut?" Erica wasn't sure whether to be terrified or amazed, but was pretty sure she swung more toward terror in that moment. Had they been safely in the temple, she'd probably have been more on the amazed end of the spectrum.

"Not all, but enough you have to be careful of all." A little giggle jumped out of Jilly. She ignored it. "I wasn't careful. I'm making mistakes." Another mostly ignored chuckle.

Erica felt a laugh bubbling up her throat, too. She swallowed it hard and refocused on the text, making a concerted effort *not* to touch the ink.

"What happens if you get blood on the pages?" Erica had been training enough to know that blood and magic mixed sometimes. In weird ways. And a *lot* of the books they delt with were magic on one level or another. Not just books with knowledge from strange realms in strange languages. Actual magical stuff.

"Probably nothing good. Better not to risk it. Don't remember anything about blood and the book, but you never know."

"Was afraid of that." Another laugh tightened in her chest. She clamped her mouth shut until it subsided. Then she focused on the page again.

And there! There. Something in all those runic-looking lines. A word. A word she could just about read. The ink winked and twinkled faintly, even in the diffuse light coming through her shirt, but not enough to prevent her seeing it.

"There's something there," she said, her voice tight and intent. "Almost...almost got it."

Another laugh burst from her. So loud it startled her and

she slapped a hand over her mouth, dropping enough of her shirt to let bright sunshine under the slim canopy.

A bright flash of reflected light off the page made her squint. She struggled to raise the shirt again, but Jilly stopped her with a sound that was half-laugh, half-grunt.

"Leave it. Look."

Erica squinted at the book. And there it was. The runes resolving themselves into words she could almost read. Several Earth languages all at once, but words she knew.

"Can you read it yet?" she asked Jilly.

"Shh." Jilly leaned closer to the book. Her finger still dripped a few drops of blood into the sand, but she ignored it.

Erica wanted to put something on that cut, but first they had to break whatever curse or spell or whatever had got the cats all napping in ancient sand boxes.

She blinked. Sand boxes? Like a sandbox, but sort of reversed with the boxes in the sand instead of the sand inside the box. Was that supposed to be, like…a joke? A pun? Did whoever put the book in this realm even know what a sandbox was?

Deciding it had to be a weird coincidence, she refocused on the writing. More of the words were in languages she could read now. But she was only picking up random words, not full sentences or anything that made sense.

Fire. Weeds. Jingle. Bells. Death.

That last was worrying.

She spotted boxes, sit, claws, angry, and destiny. Then something about…cats?

"Why am I seeing the word cat all over this passage?"

It was in different languages from different countries in their realm: gato, cattus, katze, chat, kedi, neko—Erica couldn't read Japanese, but she knew the Japanese word for cat because a colleague at the university specialized in

Japanese history and she collected cat statues—a few more words she thought might be cat if she just read those languages.

None of the passages with the word in it resolved into full sentences for her. But there were definitely cats all over the page.

She chuckled again, but ignored the reaction. "Is this some kind of cat book?"

"It's actually referencing the Destiny Cats, but… I'm not sure why?"

"Destiny Cats?"

"Our cats. The guardians. Some cultures call them Destiny Cats."

"Why? And why didn't I know about that? And when was someone going to tell me?"

Jilly didn't even glance up from the book. "It's a good name. Never came up. Would have told you eventually when it did. Like now."

"Fair. Is this like…a trap for them?" She looked around again. At all the cats sleeping inside the various boxes, with tendril vines covering them, locking them into the boxes. At Galahad and Memnon now staring at them like Erica and Jilly were some sort of empty spot near the ceiling. That sort of stare that made you think the cats had seen a ghost and were watching it.

Not a good image. She really hoped they weren't looking at ghosts.

"Well, they would be with the guardian coming to retrieve the book," Jilly said. "The people who put it here were trying to hide it, and they'd done a very good job. They didn't want it pulled out of the desert."

"So…maybe we should leave it? After we free the cats, that is. Maybe we shouldn't bring it back to the temple."

"The reason I could find it now, the reason I finally uncovered the clues to get us here..." Jilly finally looked up. "That means either the Wraith-sworn or the Elder-sworn have discovered where it is and are on their way here to get it. It will always be more dangerous in their hands than ours. We wouldn't be here if the book wasn't going to be safer in the temple."

"But why set up protections against the cats and not the Wraiths and Elders?"

"Maybe they couldn't? Maybe the ones who originally hid the book thought the cats and the temple were the greater danger? We'd have to ask them. And they're long gone. This book has been hidden for several millennia." Her attention had already returned to the book as she finished. "Okay. I think I have it. Get ready."

"Get ready? Get ready for what?"

Jilly laughed, but Erica couldn't tell if it was real humor or the weird laughter the book seemed to be causing.

Jilly collected some sand in her hand with the cut finger and held it up. She murmured some words from the book, though too quietly for Erica to hear. She wasn't even sure what language. She looked at the page Jilly stared out, trying to see what her aunt saw.

And image rose up from the page, flashing forward like it would hit Erica. The 3D effect so sudden, Erica dropped backward from the book. The image continued to hover over the page even though she was no longer looking directly at the page. It was a sort of spherical shape, a shimmery gold color, not too different from the sand, and at Jilly's next word, the sphere shivered.

A jingling sound echoed around the dunes, loud enough Erica gasped and covered her ears.

Oh no. If that hurt her, that had to hurt the cats. One lone howl confirmed her worry.

Jilly said something else from the book, letting the sand on her hand slide down to the ground. Erica was relieved to see no more blood dripping from her finger, but something about the way the sand slid off Jilly's palm felt ominous.

Another shiver through the sphere and it jingled again. A booming sort of sound that literally made the ground shake.

Jilly pressed her lips together, her face screwing up tight as she glanced across the dunes. She shook her head and read one final passage.

The sphere let loose a ringing, echoing, chaotic sound that Erica felt vibrating through her bones. Even with her hands clamped over her ears, the sound set her teeth on edge and pounded against her skull like the worst hangover in the history of hangovers.

More howls and yowls from the cats. Erica looked up in time to see the vines covering the sleeping cats start to snap like broken rubber bands releasing and freeing the animals. The instant they were free, they each raced out of their box and circled up around Jilly, Erica, and the book.

The last cat to jump free was Nimue. She rose from her box, stretched, and then, as if realizing something was wrong, leapt free of the container and raced to join the others. Memnon and Galahad circled the guardians a few times and then Memnon settled at Jilly's side and Galahad at Erica's.

Jilly murmured one last word and the golden sphere sank back into the page. The jingling sound stopped. And the last of the sand slid off Jilly's palm.

A beat, two, then Erica looked around. All the cats were with them. The vines that had started to grow over them were now blackened and dead. A breeze fluttered across the dunes, shifting individual grains and moving the dead vines around.

Silence for a long moment.

Then Jilly let out a sigh. "Well. That was fun."

"Ha!" Erica said. Then realized, "Hey, I'm not laughing for no reason. That must be good, right? Did you break... whatever that was, too?"

"Must have. Still not sure what that was." Jilly flipped the book closed with her uninjured hand. "Let's get back and get this safely stored." Her gaze moved out over the desert again, her eyes narrowed.

"What are you worried about?" Erica rose and gently helped Jilly back to her feet.

"Worms and sand-dragons," Jilly murmured. "The vibration and noise..." She trailed off, her stare into the distance reminding Erica of the way Galahad and Memnon had been staring earlier.

Erica followed Jilly's gaze. A spout of sand plumed up over a distant dune. "That's bad, isn't it?"

"Yes," Jilly said. "That's bad."

"Run?"

"Run."

They both turned and tore off in the direction of the tree, the cats swarming up around them. Memnon raced to the front of the group, taking the lead, while Galahad fell back to cover the rear of the group.

Erica nearly slowed, nearly fell into step with Galahad, as much to make sure he was okay as to protect the others.

But Jilly grabbed her arm and tugged her on. "Don't slow down. Don't look back."

"Don't say that! Why did you say that?" Because the very first thing Erica wanted to do now was look back.

She resisted the urge, but only barely. Keeping her head down, clenching her shirt in one hand, she ran across the dunes as fast as she'd run to catch the cats. The sun baked her exposed skin, but she didn't feel like she had the time to pause and put her shirt back on. Not when, faintly and at the very edge of her hearing, she heard a thud, like something heavy hitting the sand.

The tree came into view just as she was starting to wheeze. She'd gotten into better shape since Jilly had revealed this destiny to her, but running over sand dunes underneath a scorching sun had not been in the training regime.

Note to self: add it to the list.

She gulped in air and tried not to slow down. The tree was there, in view, so close. Just a few more hundred yards and they'd be there.

She wasn't sure a single palm tree in the middle of all this sand qualified as *safe*, but it was the way home. And she really wanted to get out of this desert before whatever was making that thudding noise behind them got close enough for her to see.

Despite her desperate need to turn and *look* at what was approaching, she managed to follow Jilly's warning and didn't. It took a great deal of effort. That saying about curiosity and cats…? Yeah, she was that. She was the cat. And she was really afraid if she didn't heed Jilly's warning, she'd end up dead.

The thud got louder. A sound like a dinosaur bellow from a movie rose not far behind her. That sound made her blood run cold. She tried to run faster, but her limbs felt like rubber.

Screams and shouts around her. She realized some of the cats had returned to their human forms. All of them shouting and pushing to reach the tree before…

Another loud bellow, so close Erica screamed.

Then a strong arm wrapped around her waist, practically

lifting her off her feet, and the last dozen yards to the tree flashed by.

When the shade of the tree washed over her, Erica shudder. Sweat dripped over her skin, blurring her vision. But when she looked up, Galahad stood next to her, his arm around her waist, his scowl fiercer than she'd ever seen.

And she'd never been so grateful to see his scowl in her life.

"You okay?" she said, wheezing as she tried to catch her breath.

"Be better once we're home." He looked out across the desert. This time, Erica followed his gaze and risked that forbidden look back.

Yup.

She shouldn't have done that.

CHAPTER SEVEN

*E*rica watched a creature that she could only describe as an oversized orange cylinder rising up out of the pink sands, high enough to block the sun and cast them in deep shadows. The shade did not compensate for the overwhelming fear that tore through her.

Whatever the creature was, it was huge. It had a circular mouth filled with teeth. And it was entirely too close to their cover under the palm tree. A palm tree that was their gateway home.

Erica watched the thing hover above them, and beyond being eaten in that giant mouth, another terrifying thought occurred to her. "What if it smashes the tree?"

"Harder to do that you might think," Galahad said. "But if it managed it, we'd be trapped here."

"We should get back now, then. Before…that."

"Through the tree," Jilly ordered, her voice snapping out. "Now!"

The creature stopped rising and suddenly started falling, slamming into the sand hard enough to make the ground shake. Erica grabbed Galahad for balance, though he was still holding on to her. The ground rumbled and the sands shifted and a deep vibration moved through her feet.

She exchanged a look with Galahad. Then everyone was moving. Fast. Into the tree gate.

Jilly and Memnon made all the other guards go through first, and Erica echoed Jilly's insistence when Nimue wanted to stay and make sure Erica got through. Nester had to practically carry the young cat to make her go first. When only the four of them remained, Erica still refused to go until Jilly was through. And Galahad wouldn't go until Memnon had.

As they watched Memnon disappear into the tree trunk, the ground behind them shivered and shook again. Erica could feel the sand moving, hear the dunes rumbling. The air filled with a spicy, salty scent she could taste. Deeper shade rose up over them.

Erica and Galahad looked over their shoulders as the body of one of the creatures rose up so close, she couldn't see around it. So close that if it dropped down, it was going to fall right on top of them. And that was if it didn't open that mouth full of teeth and devour them.

"Go! Now!" Galahad grabbed her around the waist again and lunged toward the tree.

She was already jumping at the palm's trunk when he did.

Their momentum sent them tumbling into the portal just as she heard a thumping sound behind her. Then the darkness closed around her and the weird, whooshing journey took her.

When they exited the portal through the cat tree inside the temple, Erica tripped out, stumbling as if she was still moving from her jump to get away from whatever the hell that creature had been. Galahad caught her and kept her from hitting the ground, though they both had to take a few extra steps to catch their balance.

She blinked up at him, knowing her eyes were wide and her pulse was still pounding from the fear. "Thanks," she said.

"You're welcome." His voice was very deep.

"Bit scary, that, huh?" She tried to smile.

He didn't smile back.

"You okay? After..." She waved a hand. He'd been caught in the spell or whatever it was that Jilly had had to break. Had it left any residual effects?

"Been better." He glanced away. "I nearly failed you."

"No." She forced his face around with a hand to his jaw. The muscles under her fingertips jumped. "No," she said firmly. "That spell or whatever was *specifically* made for you and the other cats. There was nothing you could have done."

"Memnon wasn't affected."

"He's been at this longer, right? But even Nester got overwhelmed. They all did." She lowered her voice and nodded to the others.

Jilly and Memnon were at the table in the center of the temple floor, looking at the book they'd retrieved, their heads bent together as they talked too quietly to be heard. The other guard-cats were sitting on some of the cushions scattered around the temple or had collapsed onto the ground. Nester spoke softly with Nimue who looked as upset as Galahad did. All of Jilly's guard-cats looked exhausted.

"Would you blame any of them for getting caught?" she asked him quietly. "Nimue? She got caught first. Do you blame her?"

"Of course not," he said, his voice gruff. "But she's also young and new to this."

"And you're new to being the librarian and my guard," she murmured. She lowered her voice even more when she said, "And Memnon raced off to save his son. You realize he left Jilly to save you, right? And he's in love with her. He still raced off to save you. You weren't the only one that didn't… stick to a schedule of duty." She frowned a little at that turn of phrase and hoped he understood what she was trying to say. "What I mean is, you can stop beating yourself up. We're all fine now." She tried a little smile. "In hindsight, that'll probably have been fun, right?"

He just stared at her.

"Okay. Yeah, you're right. Not fun. Not fun at all. What was that creature? Was that a sand-dragon?"

"That was a worm."

Her stomach bottomed out and her knees wobbled. Galahad tightened his hold on her, keeping her from falling.

They both seemed to realize at the exact same moment that she was still just wearing her bra and had her shirt clenched in her hand. His arms were very warm against her bare skin.

"Why don't you have a shirt on?" he asked, keeping his gaze very carefully on hers.

"Was using it for shade, so we could see the book." She nodded, pursed her lips, tried to ignore the heat crawling across her cheeks.

"Did it work?"

"Mmhmm," she said. "Mostly."

"Good." There was a distinct twitch to his mouth that might have been a smile.

She narrowed her eyes at him in warning. That only made the almost-smile worse.

"You probably got a sunburn, you know," he said. "You're going to need to put something on that."

"Sure. Sure. I'll…uh. Yeah. I'll do that when we get home."

"You have after-sun lotion at home? In Chicago?"

"There are stores," she said defensively. Until she realized he was trying to joke. To tease. And he so rarely did that, so rarely relaxed around her enough to joke with her, she laughed.

It was a normal laugh. A natural laugh. Not that weird giggle caused by the book. And it felt good.

"Pretty exciting for your first retrieval," Galahad said as he slowly loosened his hold on her and she stepped away from him.

"Exciting. Yeah. That's what that was. Exciting." She dragged her shirt back over her head before she had time to think about the fact that she'd been running around in just her bra for a while now. Good thing it was a pretty bra and not one of her ratty ones.

"You did good," Jilly called from the table. "Both of you." She gestured at the book. "This is one of the dangerous ones. If you hadn't noticed."

There was a general murmuring and groaning from the cats.

"And now we can keep it here safely, study it."

"You sure you want to study it?" Erica asked, approaching the table, and the book, cautiously. "That weird unnatural laughing..."

"The sound of bells..." Galahad added.

"None of it was good. You really want to risk that happening again?"

"We'll take precautions," Jilly said. She exchanged a look with Memnon. "And...maybe wait on the study part for a bit. It's just good to have the book safely here in the temple."

She looked around at all the exhausted cats, most of whom were in their human forms. At Erica and Galahad. Then she and Memnon exchanged another looked and he raised his brows. Jilly did a little shoulder dip of a shrug. Memnon smiled.

"Anyone want a drink?" he asked.

A general chorus of cheers went up, echoing off the high roof of the pyramid.

As Memnon and Nester went to a chest near the back wall, Jilly joined Erica where Erica was taking off her scabbard belt and gently laying her sword aside. She'd pretty much forgotten she'd had the sword, except for shoving it out of the way when she'd dropped into the sand.

She gave it a look, then looked at Jilly. "Would this have helped against one of those worms?" She nodded at Jilly's sword, now laying gently on the table, still inside its scabbard. "Would yours?"

"Alendrial is a very good sword. But nothing can penetrate the hide of one of those worms. Running was our only option."

Erica tried not to shiver. "Good to know. Good to know."

"You okay after all that?"

"I think so." She leaned against a shelf stacked with rolled papyrus documents. "Is it always like that? Always so... So close to potential disaster?"

"Always? No." Jilly shrugged. "Often enough? Yes. And no, it doesn't get any easier."

"How have you done this over and over again for all these years?"

"It's my duty. My destiny. One I accepted decades ago." She frowned a little and pushed a strand of hair off Erica's forehead. "But I remember the first retrieval. Not quite as dramatic as yours. But not easy either. It would have been easy to quit at that stage."

"I can't quit, though, can I? If I fail...disaster." A war

between the Wraiths and the Elders that would destroy all the realms. That was why they did what they did.

"Doesn't mean quitting doesn't cross your mind." Jilly ducked her head a little to meet Erica's gaze. "Do you want to quit?"

Erica glanced around the room, smiling a little at the cats as they passed around a few bottles of what she suspected was fermented milk because they had weird taste in what they considered alcoholic drinks. There'd be wine somewhere over there for her and Jilly.

Erica's gaze landed on Galahad. And Nimue. And Nester. The two older cats had gathered around Nimue and were giving her reassuring pats and bumps. And for the first time since they'd walked through the portal, Nimue was smiling.

She was new too, Erica thought. Both of them so new to this. But *this* was so important.

Her gaze danced over Galahad again, and he caught her look. His small smile came and went quickly. But it was enough.

"I was absolutely terrified out there," Erica said, turning back to Jilly. "But I don't want to quit. I can do this."

Jilly grinned and pulled her into a hug. "I know you can. It's why you were chosen." She pulled back and patted Erica on the shoulders. "Now. Let's get drunk and come up with all the demands you're going to put to your department head at your rescheduled meeting."

Erica snort-laughed at that, but let her aunt pull her to the guards. And the waiting bottles of wine.

As they passed the table, Erica swore she heard a very faint jingling from the book. Almost too quiet for her to hear. She glanced back at it, but it was exactly where Jilly had left it. And the claw marks in the front of the book looked a lot less red now.

A moment later the sound died away completely. Erica let out a long breath and hurried to take one of the offered bottles of wine.

That was one book she could definitely wait to study.

In fact, that was one book she might never want to read again.

THANK YOU

Thank you for reading Haunts and Howls and Jesters Bells! I hope you enjoyed this latest Haunts and Howls collection. I definitely had fun writing these stories. And now you can see what I meant by my weird sense of humor. If this is your first Haunts and Howls collection, I hope you'll consider picking up the others. Also, if you'd just like to read any of the individual stories on their own, most are now out as standalone eBooks (or will be soon).

For more on my fiction, please consider joining my newsletter. You'll get news, updates, release information, excerpts, occasional cover reveals, discounts to my fan store, and two free stories exclusive to my newsletter—one in my Cary Redmond urban fantasy series, and one in my Tiger Shifters paranormal romance series.

If you prefer, you can check on my latest releases at my fan store at KatSimonsBooks, on my website, or follow my author pages at BookBub or your favorite book vendor.

Thanks again for reading!

THE TROUBLE WITH BLACK CATS AND DEMONS

EXCERPT

CHAPTER ONE

"Not again." Cary Redmond ducked as another fireball clipped over her head. "You don't think fireballs are a bit over the top," she shouted up at the ceiling then had to duck again as a dagger whispered past her ear.

Close. Her heart pounded. Way too close.

She needed to find the damned cat and get out of here. She scanned the apartment from her dubious cover behind a table piled high with unopened mail. Fireballs, daggers, gusts of preternatural wind, freezing hail, and the occasional lightning bolt dropped around her, roaring through the living room in a bright cacophony of magical mayhem.

The lightning bolts flashing in the small confines were pretty spectacular. If they hadn't been trying to fry her, she might have enjoyed the show.

"Jaxer, I'm going to kill you for this."

Normally, this kind of thing was just a part of her job. She was a Protector and literally got paid to run around keeping people safe, mostly from magical bad guys. Not that she'd asked for the job, but that was another story. It *was* her job, so she faced off against dangerous stuff because the Nags—her bosses—told her to.

Tonight, however, was not an official assignment. Tonight, she was just doing a favor for her demented faery mentor. The bastard knew exactly how to get to her. All he had to do was mention a defenseless little black kitty cat and she was done for. How could she refuse to help a kitty? People did rotten things to black cats on Halloween.

Except Jaxer had forgotten to warn her about the fireballs.

She screeched through her teeth and dove behind the couch as one of the aforementioned fireballs barreled toward her. She cursed Jaxer as she took a quick look under the couch for the cat. Where the hell was it?

She'd called out to it when she'd first entered the apartment but hadn't gotten any irate kitty responses. After her lurching hunt of the living room and kitchen, the only place left was the bedroom.

She pulled in a deep breath as she contemplated the long space of unprotected ground between her hiding spot behind the couch and the bedroom door. Once she found the cat, this would be easier. When she was actively protecting something, very little of the magical dangers could get to her, and nothing deadly would touch her. She just had to *find* the cat first. And quickly. They had to be out of this cursed apartment before midnight. Before the wizard got home and all hell broke loose.

Again.

She ducked flying objects and ran to the bedroom, squealing when a lightning bolt hit the ground right behind her. Crossing her fingers that there were no nasty spells waiting for her, she lunged through the half-open door and cringed in anticipation of magical repercussions as she fell onto a red-carpeted floor. She held perfectly still, waiting.

Nothing. She let out a breath and pushed herself up onto her hands and knees, shaking her head. All this for a cat. That bastard Jaxer had a lot to answer for.

She rose to a crouch, trying to calm her racing pulse, and froze.

In front of her sat a huge bed, which she barely noticed because the naked man lying in the middle of the enormous mattress stopped her heart.

Holy shit.

He was absolutely magnificent. Tanned skin, well-defined muscles, thick, black hair hanging down over his forehead. He was lying against a giant headboard with his head hanging forward so she couldn't get a good look at his face, but his golden eyes seemed to glow up at her from under his brows. Piercing and stunning and breath-stealing.

Cary swallowed. Hard. Because even the captivating gold of his eyes wasn't enough to keep her gaze from wandering over the breadth of his naked chest, the corded muscles of his shoulders and arms, the flat expanse of his stomach. It took a great deal of will power not to follow the line of dark hair arrowing down his abdomen…lower.

The man straightened and Cary heard the clink of chains at the same time as she got a look at his neck—and the thick collar covering most of it.

What the hell had Jaxer gotten her into?

"Who're you?" she asked, breathless and embarrassed.

"Who are you?"

His voice carried a deep reverberation that made her spine tingle. Oh boy.

"I'm looking for a black cat," she said, knowing the explanation sounded inane. Jaxer had told her about Sheldon the Wizard, but this? This was something else all together. What was this guy doing here? He wasn't Sheldon, she was sure of it. But then who was he? And where was the cat?

She blinked and a black leopard lay on the bed where the man had been. She sucked in a sharp breath, blinked again. And the man was back.

"Whoa." Cary swallowed. "*You're* the black cat I came to rescue?"

Oh, she really was going to kill Jaxer now. He hadn't said anything about a fully grown man who happened to be a leopard shapeshifter. He'd made sure she thought she was after a little, harmless kitty cat, not a deadly dangerous big cat who shifted into a beautiful, naked, very large man.

The faery was dead. Not that she knew how to kill him, but that was beside the point.

"Jaxer sent you?" The man's eyes narrowed and his features took on a dangerous edge. He hissed a curse under his breath and shook his head. "Stupid."

"Hey!" She stood, the better to face his gorgeous disgust. No one should look that good while insulting you. "You could have done worse, buddy."

She took a step toward the bed, wiping damp palms on her jeans. The chains she'd heard earlier linked the collar on his neck to the headboard, which was brass and made-up of a scrawl of symbols she didn't recognize but looked like they might mean something if she stared at them long enough. He wasn't bound anywhere else that she dared peek, and the chains appeared flimsy enough. So obviously the power keeping him confined was in the collar.

"What is that?" She gestured with her head toward the thick band of metal.

"A binding ring," he said slowly, as if speaking to a child.

She frowned, both at his tone and the news. "But you just shifted."

"It's been designed to contain both my forms. Any other questions before you get me out of here?"

"Yeah, what crawled up your butt and put you in such a pissy mood?"

"Being held captive for sacrifice by a wizard and having a child sent to rescue me has dampened my day a bit," he said.

She grinned and enjoyed watching his eyes narrow suspiciously. "Child, huh? You know, at my age that's a compliment."

"How old could you be? Twenty?"

She shook her head. She'd actually turned thirty-one last April. But when she got tricked into becoming a Protector at twenty-five, she'd stopped aging at a normal rate. One of the few things about the job that didn't irritate her.

She took a quick moment to glance around the rest of the room. The red carpet wasn't the only gaudy element. Lots of black leather covered the walls and an animal skinned rug, which she was afraid to think about too closely given the captive on the overlarge bed, was tossed across the floor in front of what she thought might be a closet. A wood and metal trunk sat against one wall, red silk drapes covered the single window, and the overhead light was covered by thick, dark metal chains which gave the room strange shadows.

Fortunately, there were no nasty attack spells in here, which meant Sheldon the Wizard didn't want his captive accidentally hurt by a stray lightning bolt. That worked in her favor, giving her time to solve the binding ring problem without being pelted by hail.

Though even if there had been spells in here, now that she was officially protecting someone, she could keep them both safe.

She did wonder why Sheldon would care if his shape shifting captive got hurt before the midnight sacrifice.

Obviously, he didn't want him dead. You couldn't sacrifice something that was already dead. But an additional warning spell in here probably wouldn't have killed his prisoner. Maybe. If Sheldon had enough control.

If he didn't, and was as powerful as Jaxer claimed, they really needed to get out of here. Fast.

She eased up to the bedside, still leery of traps, and leaned in close to the leopard man, trying to ignore the yummy, stomach-fluttering male scent of him as she studied the binding ring. It was a thick band of silver and copper intertwined in a complex pattern of twists and turns. Over the silver, tiny runic symbols danced and shimmered so they were nearly impossible to read.

"Oh good," she said, "a hard one."

The prisoner shivered, a low growl rising from his throat. The sound made Cary's heartbeat jump.

Speaking of hard ones.

She could feel his glare on the side of her face, but she resisted looking. She had other things to worry about at the moment.

Like how the hell she was going to get this damned magical containment brace off his neck without alerting the entire mystical neighborhood.

"You did that on purpose," the man snarled.

"Huh?" She glanced at him. "What are you talking about?"

"Don't breathe on me again," he said.

She scowled. "What am I supposed to do? Hold my breath until I get your collar off? Just relax, big guy. You'll be out of here in a minute." To herself, she mumbled, "Wouldn't have gotten this much grief from a proper black cat."

"You some kind of witch?"

"No." After a moment, she sighed and shook her head.

"Well, there's no help for it. I'm gonna have to use brute force. It'll take too long to get this off subtly."

"We don't have much time. It's nearly midnight now."

"Gee, really?"

He ignored her sarcasm. "Brute force?"

"Hold onto your valuable body parts," she said and tried not to think about his exposed valuable parts. Then she wrapped her hands around the collar, easing her fingers gently under so the backs pressed against his neck. His skin was warm and another shiver danced down her spine.

"Wait."

She met his gaze.

"What the hell are you doing? If I can't break that with my bare hands, you can't—"

He stopped short when she tugged and the collar came away with a quiet click.

"I'm not without some talent," she murmured.

"Who *are* you?"

"Come on. We have to get you out of here. I just made a lot of magical noise with that little stunt."

"Hold on."

He grabbed her hand. The feel of his warm palm wrapped around her fingers sent tiny sparks of electricity dancing over her skin. He dropped his hold, but she saw his eyes widen with the same shock she felt. He inhaled deeply, and against her will, she watched the strong muscles of his chest rise and fall.

"What's your name?" he asked.

"Cary."

"Cary. I'm Deacon."

"Nice to meet you." Did that sounded as stupid to him as it did to her given the circumstances?

He smiled, a slow, deadly grin that made her pulse race. "Nice to meet you, too."

She blinked and shook her head. "Come on, Deacon. We need to move."

As he slid to the edge of the mattress, Cary turned her back to avoid embarrassing them both—despite the temptation to look over every inch of him. The sound of material moving over skin behind her didn't help curb her less polite impulses, though, so she hurried to the door to see how the lightning bolts and fireballs were doing.

Slipping into his jeans, Deacon watched the woman as she peeked around the edge of the doorframe at the living room and the still popping spells Sheldon had set to keep help from reaching him.

She wasn't the rescue he'd been expecting. He'd expected the damned faery to come himself.

Jaxer had convinced him to let the wizard "capture" him, so they could find out *why* Sheldon was kidnapping shifters. They'd only found a few of Sheldon's victims—their bodies anyway. And they'd been little more than desiccated husks. The rest of the missing shifters... Even their bodies had vanished.

Wizards didn't typically go after shapeshifters for sacrifice. They were too hard to contain, and most of them didn't have the kind of magical energy an average human wizard could absorb through ceremonial magic. Shapeshifting wasn't typically magic. It was just a species trait.

Deacon knew none of the shifters killed so far had had any actual magic. He was a different case, but he was pretty sure Sheldon didn't know that. Jaxer did, which was why he'd come to Deacon in the first place, and Deacon had felt obliged to help even though none of the shifters taken had been leopards.

He suppressed an irritated growl. This was the last time he'd let the faery use him for bait. He'd been chained to that fucking bed all day with no sign of help. Then Jaxer went and made things worse by sending in this...woman to rescue him instead of coming himself. How dare he endanger someone else when this crusade against Sheldon was his own personal business? Bad enough he dragged Deacon into it.

But as Deacon watched the woman straighten away from the doorframe when a lightning bolt flashed, he realized there *was* something about her. He couldn't deny the power she must have to break through the binding ring. Yet she looked and smelled like a normal, human woman.

Her light brown hair hung in long ponytail her back over a battered brown leather jacket. She wore jeans, hiking boots, and a purple t-shirt with a glittery Happy Halloween emblazoned over a maniacally grinning jack-o-lantern. Her blue eyes had sparkled when he'd called her a child, then flashed with irritation when he'd insulted her. And for reasons he couldn't quite understand, he'd found it hard to look away from her, especially when she'd knelt next to him on the bed.

Something about her...something about her scent tugged at his instincts.

Who the hell was she? *What* was she? She had to be more than human, but none of his sense picked up anything particularly preternatural about her. So where did all that power come from?

Jaxer had some serious explaining to do.

Deacon shook off his preoccupation and walked up behind her to stare at the living room over her head. Black scorch marks marred the hardwood floors, and a layer of frost covered one side table. The air was heavy with electricity and the smell of burning ozone.

Despite the multiple magical eruptions, the apartment was in remarkably good shape. As he watched, a dagger flew toward the bedroom, dropped harmlessly a foot from the doorway, and disappeared as if it hadn't existed.

Clever. Less clean up. And a testament to Sheldon's power.

He couldn't blame Jaxer for being worried about the little shit. But given a choice, Deacon would have taken a more… active approach to getting rid of the wizard.

Unfortunately, and he was reluctant to admit this even to himself, his approach probably would have gotten him killed. The bastard wizard was powerful. How Sheldon managed to be so powerful at his age was a mystery. But maybe that was the reason Jaxer was so obsessed with finding out the *whys* behind Sheldon's actions.

If Deacon got out of this apartment alive, he'd ask the faery. In the meantime, he and this very human woman in front of him had to navigate the bespelled living room and get away before Sheldon got back.

Deacon drew in a slow breath and was hit again by Cary's scent. Vanilla and cinnamon. And something else. Something that shot jolts of lust and need through his gut, making him lean closer to her just so he could feel the heat of her skin. He felt a possessive growl rising in his throat and swallowed it back, fisting his hands by his side to keep from reaching for her.

What the hell? He had more control that this. A lot more. He had to or people got killed. Resisting a woman, even one that smelled like heaven, had never been a problem before. With Cary, it took an effort to resist pulling her close and burying his face in her neck to soak up her essence.

If he didn't know better, he'd think she was a witch, casting a lust spell on him.

His nostrils flared. That scent of hers...

It reached down inside him, calling to a deep instinct. As he breathed her in, his leopard whispered, *Mine.*

Out in the living room, wind-lashed hail whipped toward the bedroom without actually coming through the doorway. And behind that, a lightning bolt sizzled the floor.

"Sheldon didn't make this easy," he said, quirking a brow when she jumped at the sound of his voice.

"Are you dressed?" she asked without turning around.

He couldn't help smiling at the slight panic in her voice. "Yes."

"Okay. Stick close. Stay behind me and don't try to dodge around me. Got it? That's how we'll get out of here alive."

He frowned down at the top of her head. She must have some pretty powerful shields to get through that mess. But she wasn't a witch?

He grunted a noncommittal response, and she swung around to face him. The flash of heat in her eyes made his pulse kick.

"Listen, buddy," she said, her chin tucked back as she glared at him, "if you don't let me protect you, we're both dead. Okay? Don't go trying to be a hero. Just stay close and let me do what I came here to do."

She mumbled something unflattering under her breath as she turned back to the living room, and he had to fight a completely irrational urge to kiss her.

Over the course of the long day, with no sign of help from Jaxer, he'd had to face the possibility of his own death. His reaction to Cary might be a result of that, a need to reaffirm he was alive.

EXCERPT

But as he breathed in the heady scent of her again, he wondered…

**Don't Miss
The Trouble with Black Cats and Demons
Cary Redmond, Book One**

BOOKS BY KAT SIMONS

Haunts and Howls Collections

Haunts and Howls and Guardian Spells

Haunts and Howls Where Demons Dwell

Haunts and Howls and Jesters Bells

The Cary Redmond Series

* The Trouble Black Cats and Demons * The Trouble with Ghouls and Serial Killers * The Trouble with Leopard Queens and Shifter Wars * The Trouble with Baby Gods and Vampires * The Trouble with Magic and Faery Curses * The Trouble with Wizards and Old Enemies * The Trouble with Death and Demon Gods

The Cary Redmond Series Box Set Books 1-3

Cary Redmond Short Stories

* When Cary Met Jaxer * When Cary Met Pickles * When Cary Met Marianne * When Cary Met Lucy * When Cary Met Angie * Cary and Deacon (Try to) Go on a Date * Date Night Take Two * Third Date's the Charm * Cary vs the Goblin King * Dinner with the Joneses * Cary and the Cursed Jack-O'-Lantern * Cary and the Demon Witch * Cary Goes to Hawaii * Cary Holidays * Cary and Dragons and Goblins * Cary's Galentine's Day * Cary at the Haunt and Howl * Cary's Leprechaun Troubles

* Cary's Beltane Night Out

When Cary Met the Good Guys (Collection 1)

Dates, Dinners, and Other Disasters (Collection 2)

Witches and Weavers and Ghosts, Oh Boy (Collection 3)

A Very Cary Holiday (Collection 4)

Romancing the Leopard: A Tiger Shifters-Cary Redmond Crossover Novel

Tiger Shifters Series

* Once Upon a Tiger * Along Came a Tiger * Here There Be Tigers * Her Tiger To Take * To Tempt a Tiger * Down Will Come Tiger * To Catch a Tiger * What a Tiger Wants

* Taming Her Tiger

Tiger Shifters Series Vol 1 (Books 1 - 3)

Tiger Shifters Series Vol 2 (Books 4 - 6)

Seven Families Series

Wolf Family

Darkness in Stone

Redemption in Stone

Fated in Stone

Demon Witch Series

Howling Dreadful

Moonlit Strange

Bone Lantern Witch

Spiderweb Witch

Storm Shadow Witch

Joan of Kerry Series

Joan of Kerry: Joan and the Abhartach

Joan and the Leprechaun

Joan and the Kraken

*Tombstone Wizard * The Unshattered Sword * Destiny Through the Cats Eyes * Going Out of Business: Everything's for Sale * Anger Management * Demonic Dates * Friday's Curious Shop * The Museum of Small Art's Everyman * Burning Inside a Stone Circle (*coming soon*)

MORE BOOKS BY KAT SIMONS

Pick Your Genre Collections

Who Steals a Dragon

Contemporary Romances

Designed for You
Poinsettias and Possibilities

Mystery and Thrillers

Ross and O'Neill Adventures
Galileo's Pendulum

Percy James Mysteries
Movies May Murder
Cookies Can't Crime
Diamonds Do Damage
Coming 2023

ABOUT THE AUTHOR

Kat Simons earned her Ph.D. in animal behavior, working with animals as diverse as dolphins and deer. She brought her experience and knowledge of biology to her paranormal romance and urban fantasy fiction, where she delights in taking nature and turning it on its ear. She writes urban fantasy, contemporary fantasy, and paranormal romance in series which combine action adventure, the otherworldly, and a frequent dose of sexy romance.

The latest book in her bestselling romantic urban fantasy series about Protector Cary Redmond, The Trouble with Death and Demon Gods, is also out now. As are the newest stories in the romantic urban fantasy Demon Witch series, including the first "meet cute" for Angie and her demon hunter boyfriend Sebastian in the novella *Howling Dreadful*.

The novel Darkness in Stone launches the newest paranormal romance series for Kat, following the exploits and loves of the Seven Families of monster hunters. The first trilogy follows the Wolf Family, as our heroes and heroines struggle to win their fated mates while fending off deadly monsters bent on destroying the world.

For something a little different, Kat also publishes fantasy, science fiction, and the occasional hockey romance under the name Isabo Kelly (https://www.isabokelly.com).

After traveling the world, living in places like Hawaii, Germany, and Ireland, Kat now lives in New York City with her family and a library's worth of books.

For more on Kat and her future books

Website: https://www.katsimons.com/
Newsletter: https://bit.ly/KatSimonsNewsletter

Kat Simons Bookstore
https://tanddpublishingbookstore.com

Social Media
Facebook Page: https://www.facebook.com/KatSimonsAuthor
BookBub: https://www.bookbub.com/authors/kat-simons
Instagram: https://www.instagram.com/isabokelly/
Twitter: https://twitter.com/IsaboKelly

Don't miss the latest Kat Simons
news, updates, excerpts, cover reveals, and more!
All new subscribers get two newsletter exclusive stories.

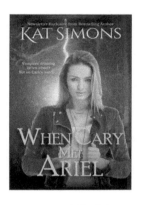

Join Now!
https://bit.ly/KatSimonsNewsletter

Enjoy all of the Haunts and Howls Collections

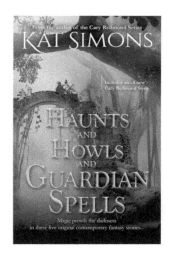

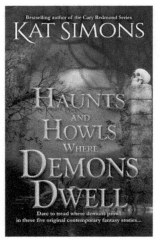

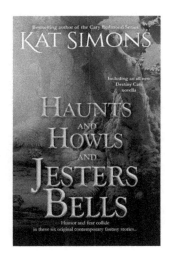

Out Now!

Milton Keynes UK
Ingram Content Group UK Ltd.
UKHW010634271123
433341UK00001B/51